Deep River, Lawd

Jean E. Holmes

Pacific Press Publishing Association
Boise, Idaho
Oshawa, Ontario, Canada

Edited by Jerry D. Thomas
Designed by Dennis Ferree
Cover art by Mark Stutzman
Typeset in 10/12 Century Schoolbook

Library of Congress Cataloging-in-Publication Data:
Holmes, Jean E., 1941-
    Deep River, Lawd / Jean E. Holmes.
        p.   cm.
    ISBN 0-8163-1119-6
    1. South Carolina—History—1775–1865—Fiction. 2. Sea
Islands—History—Fiction. I. Title
PS3558.035937D44 1993
813' .54—dc20   92-31781
                                                              CIP

93 94 95 96 97 ● 5 4 3 2 1

Contents

Foreword

The Sea Islands, by the hundreds, cluster like the jewels of a necklace along the waters of the southeastern coast of the United States, from North Carolina south to Jacksonville, Florida. Many are only a few feet above sea level. All are separated from the mainland by marshes, tidal inlets, rivers, or the sea.

For centuries, however, the Sea Islanders have been separated from the rest of the country by considerably more than water. Our enduring roots lie in West Africa. From there, our ancestors were brought to work large island plantations of indigo, rice, and cotton. Isolated by geographical and cultural barriers, our resilient people have developed and maintained their own unique language and traditions.

Life has not been easy for the Sea Islanders. One of the greatest and often unrecognized problems has been a language barrier. Our beautiful tongue, known usually as Gullah in South Carolina and as Geechee in Georgia, is a musical, English-based North Atlantic Creole. The vocabulary is primarily derived from English, although the pronunciation and usage of words differ markedly from those of regular English. Numerous distinct features of the grammatical, lexical, and phonemic systems present strong evidence of West African origin. Such relationships among languages are not at all unusual. A comparable example is that of the commonly recognized and accepted relationship of the languages derived from Latin, such as Portuguese and Spanish.

It is known that our ancestors spoke various African languages, many of them mutually unintelligible. Thrown together in common holding areas and on crowded ships, often with English-speaking overseers, our people developed a common pidgin language as a means of communication.

A pidgin tongue is, by definition, a second or auxiliary language that has no native speakers. When this pidgin spoken by our people was passed on to their American-born children, however, it became the children's native or first language. Gullah is now considered a creole language by linguists.

This creole language of our ancestors has continued to expand in form and use along the southeastern coast of the United States. It remains today as a remarkable example of our now treasured Sea Island heritage. It is estimated that approximately 250,000 people continue to speak some form of Gullah. Varieties range from the "deep" conservative speech to the more Anglicized, "lightened up" versions. As with all living languages, it is a continually changing and developing tongue. We African Americans are justly proud of the remarkable beauty and endurance of this unique aspect of our cultural heritage.

In recent years, there has been a strong resurgence of interest in Gullah. Local Sea Islanders have found that when they learned to despise their way of speaking, they learned to despise their heritage and their very selves. On the other hand, when they learned that it is an actual language, that they can properly read and write it, their pride was restored in their culture and their own selves. The language has been systematically analyzed and written down.

The team of the Sea Island Translation and Literacy Project has introduced a practical orthography adapted to English. This allows Gullah speakers to quickly become fluent readers of materials written in Gullah, if those speakers are already readers of English. It also helps Gullah speakers who are just learning to read to become better readers of both Gullah and English. The team has translated two-thirds of the New Testament into Gullah and hopes to publish the New Testament in its entirety within a few years.

It has been found that having the Bible in the language of any people gives dignity to the people and their culture. Scriptures written in Gullah become personal to Sea Island readers. As God's Word is made plain, it results in changed lives.

This book, *Deep River, Lawd*, the second of a series of five by Jean Holmes, is an important contribution to a better appreciation of the Sea Island heritage and culture. Traditions are told in a fascinating form, as the ways of "we ole people" live again. The story commands the reader's attention, while at the same time clearly informing him of Sea Island history and beliefs. Most important of all is the author's meaningful portrayal of a people enduring by their strong faith in God.

Ervin L. Greene
with Claude and Pat Sharpe
Sea Island Translation and Literacy Project

Acknowledgments

My first and greatest thanks goes to the Gullah people of the South Carolina Low Country, for this is the story of their struggle against fear, slavery, and oppression. Having borne the burden of prejudice for so long, it is most understandable that they would, even today, be apprehensive of sharing their language and culture with those who might look upon such a heritage as simplistic and backward. It is, however, an inheritance worth saving and sharing, and it was in that light that I chose to take upon myself the project of writing this book.

There are others, too, who are more than deserving of my thanks. Phyllis Dolislager, who has given of herself unstintingly to critique and repeatedly proofread my sometimes halting efforts, has been an invaluable guide and friend. Claude and Pat Sharpe, linguists with the Sea Island Translation and Literacy Project, were kind enough to review an early version of the manuscript and supply me with the beautiful scriptural references from the Gullah translation of the Bible. Gullah speakers Jennye Dudley and Kathleen Daise also read through the material and aided me by critiquing both the Gullah language and culture included in this work.

Finally, I must thank my family for giving me the time and freedom to research, write, and dream. Without such generosity, this book would not have been possible.

Dedication

This book is dedicated to the memory of
Tita Heins
Gullah Speaker, Storyteller, but most of all,
Friend!

1

De Young Lambs

(1858)

God brung E people out lukka flock ob sheep. E gone befo um lukka shepud go befo e sheep tru de desat lan (Psalm 78:52).

No one saw the children as they walked through the open door of the Big House and started down the steps toward the yard. The day was warm for February, a bit of spring tugging mischievously upon winter's somber coattails. Having flung open doors and windows to let out the musty smell, the house servants caught only the brackish odor of the river and the brittle sounds of palm fronds rustling in the breeze.

The yard hands were equally unobservant. A blue sky washed clean with sunlight numbed their minds. Air smelling of tropical places intoxicated their senses. Only a retired hound who slept under the front piazza heard the tread of the children's feet as they descended the stairs. Lifting his head once, he whined, then promptly returned to his dreams, where an elusive rabbit floated beyond his reach. Thus it was that no one saw the two little girls as they wandered off toward the wide solitude of the salt marsh. As they drew closer to the marsh, Laura May remained alert to Angel's presence a few paces behind her. Stopping frequently to wait for the crippled child to catch up, Laura smiled her encouragement or reached out her hand to give some needed support. Angel struggled on, working her way around the largest clumps of grass, smashing down the smaller ones with a quick swipe from the tip of her crutch.

If someone had been standing on the second-floor piazza on this February day, he might well have smiled at the sight of these small but determined wanderers. The children crossed a muddy patch of ground, where they stopped to watch a fiddler crab push a mud ball from its hole. Then, with the salty air of the ocean breeze brushing their faces, they entered the screen of tidal marsh grass and disappeared.

A great blue heron, disturbed in the act of dislodging his supper from a brackish puddle, spread his wide wings and lifted off. His long, gangly legs trailed behind him like the knotted tail of a kite. Circling once to determine the source of such an untimely disturbance, he swooped back over his fishing grounds. There below him he spotted the two heads. One glowed auburn and gold in the afternoon sunshine as it moved smoothly through the waving grass. The other, as black as a dolphin's eye and clustered with tight ringlets, traveled with an awkward, side-to-side jerk. Deciding to try his luck in another of his favorite haunts, the heron circled toward the river. But there, too, he found only frustration. A long line of field hands, supervised by the plantation master himself, snaked its way toward the wide expanse of water. Each hand carried a stack of planks over his shoulders. A January storm had all but destroyed the dock, leaving nothing but pilings and a few twisted boards to mark where it had once stood. The master wanted it rebuilt before the planting season got into full swing.

Master Weldon loved his little girl deeply. She brought out a softness in him, which his son, Gilly, could never do. It wasn't that he loved Gilly any less. He did love his son, but some key ingredient was missing. They couldn't communicate; their thoughts and dreams seemed to be worlds apart.

With Laura May it was different. She loved to sit encircled in her father's strong arms as they rode across the fields on Diablo, the big roan horse. Gilly had always been frightened by the massive animal. Not so with Laura. She'd stroke the animal's bulging neck muscles and laugh with delight when the long hairs of its mane tickled her face. Each evening she'd wait at the top of the stairs for her father's return, then run down to him and fling herself into his arms.

Loving the child as he did, Master Weldon would have been

beside himself with worry if he knew of her wanderings on this fine February day. But though he had crossed the yard just moments after Laura and Angel had entered the field, he had failed to notice the small footprints in the soft earth beneath the hooves of his horse. Nor had the child's mother noticed her absence. Harried as usual with so many chores to oversee, the plantation mistress had spent most of the day running between the kitchen quarters and the back pantries. With pencil and pad in hand, Marian Weldon methodically ticked off the list of dry goods that her husband would have to purchase on his next trip to Beaufort. Confident that her daughter was safe in Maum Beezie's keeping, Marian had the house servants running about like a flock of chickens in a henhouse on fire.

Poor Maum Beezie, if only she had known of the impending disaster! But before the girls had so much as gotten down the front steps, she had been fast asleep in her favorite rocking chair. It was the first real rest she had had in more than three days. Dysentery was ravaging the slave quarters, and her nursing skills were in heavy demand. When, with a sigh of relief, she had dropped heavily into the rocking chair, her charges had been sleeping as only the very young and innocent can do. Content that all was well, the elderly woman allowed herself to drift into a deep and much deserved sleep.

Maum Beezie took her duties seriously, for she loved her "chilluns" as though they were her own. Indeed, Angel was her own, one generation removed. The elderly woman had stood by her daughter Melony's bed as the young woman wrestled with the final pangs of giving birth to the child. It was Maum Beezie who had lifted up the squalling infant and cut the life-sharing cord. It was she who had first looked at those tiny, twisted feet and known the anguish of ushering an imperfect infant into a world intolerant of physical variations. And it was she who had pressed Melony's eyes closed when the last breath of life had left her body without so much as a sight of the child she had borne.

But knowing nothing of the uproar that would surely ensue when their absence was discovered, the children moved on. They crossed a stretch of marsh that had dried in the warm sun only to be halted by a fence. It presented a challenge, for it was unbroken, but Laura was undaunted by such minor obstacles. Lifting her trailing skirts above her knees, she gathered them together and tucked their ends into the muslin sash that encircled her waist.

Looking back at the crippled slave child moving awkwardly behind her, the planter's daughter felt a sudden pang of guilt. It was unfair to expect so much of Angel. Beads of sweat clung to the black girl's forehead; her kinky hair lay plastered to her scalp. The sound of her breathing came in labored gasps, each one ending with a thin whistle like the sound of the wind in the tall pines. Determined to prove herself a worthy companion, Angel was valiantly ignoring her own limitations, and Laura's guilt gave way to admiration.

Knitting her brows in concentration, Laura turned to consider the offending fence. She could easily manage the climb, but what of Angel? Leaving her friend behind was entirely out of the question. "Why did they have to go and put a fence here?" she muttered in frustration. "There's not a thing that needs to be kept out."

"Mayhap sumpin' needs keepin' in," answered Angel, with a perception beyond her years.

Fences were a rare thing on these islands. Lying like a broken string of emeralds along the ragged South Carolina and Georgia coastline, the Sea Islands were cut off from the mainland by wide estuaries and deep-water channels. The vast marshes began where the rivers ended; their coarse grasses and thick mud banks formed a nearly impenetrable barrier.

Coosaw was one of the smallest of the Sea Islands, little more than a pinprick next to its neighbor to the southeast, St. Helena Island. Bordered by two wide rivers, the Morgan to the south and the Coosaw to the north, the small island was further cut off by Lucy Point Creek to the west and Parrot Creek to the east. Under such isolated conditions, there was hardly a need for fences.

The few domestic animals that Master Weldon bred were strictly beasts of burden confined to the immediate grounds around the Big House. The two exceptions to this were Diablo and Nutmeg, the latter being a marsh tacky given to Gilly when he was hardly older than Laura herself. Gilly had long since outgrown Nutmeg, but the little tacky had become a family pet, acting more like a dog than a pony.

It was Nutmeg's hoof prints that the girls followed now. The trail left by the pony overlapped the fainter marks of the two teenage boys who had come this way just an hour before. Laura smiled to herself, feeling proud that she had guessed correctly. If Gilly and his servant, Zach, were out hunting, Nutmeg would not be far behind. Like a faithful hound, he shadowed the two older boys with a persistence bred of habit.

Laura studied the fence rails, wondering how Angel could manage the climb. The upper railing was high. How had Nutmeg gotten over it? The small pony, even in his prime, could not have tackled such a jump. Yet clearly visible in the soft ground just beyond were the marks of his hooves. If it was possible for Nutmeg to negotiate the fence, then it must surely be possible for Angel.

It was the disturbed ground and broken shafts of grass that finally told the tale. Gilly and Zach must have pulled off the top railing, then replaced it before continuing on their way. Reaching up to grasp the rough pole with her small hands, Laura May pulled with all her might. Nothing happened; the rail was too heavy for her.

"Angel, can you climb through the rails?"

Angel sized up the opening and nodded her head slowly. Though she felt bone tired from the exertion of pulling herself over the rough terrain with her crutches, she refused to consider defeat. "Here, let me help." Laura reached out for one of the crutches and slid her arm under Angel's. Hobbling along in a crablike fashion, they worked themselves up to the bottom rail, slid over it in unison, and then lay giggling in the tall grasses on the opposite side.

"Where could they have gotten by now?" wondered Laura out loud. "Maybe all the way to Parrot Creek."

Angel shrugged her shoulders without answering.

"Would you like to know a secret?" Laura pressed close to Angel's ear as though the insects in the grass might overhear and betray her. "I heard Gilly and Zach talkin' 'bout a boat they've been building out there. Gilly don't want Papa to know. Papa'd be ever so angry! Don't say nothin' 'bout it, Angel, or Gilly'll be in a passel of trouble."

Angel nodded, then pulled herself to a sitting position and cupped her hands around her eyes. "Sumpin' movin' out on de riber," she said, pointing to the shimmering surface of fast-moving water that lay just beyond a thin strip of marsh grass and mud flats.

The wind had picked up, shifting from north to northeast. High, thin clouds scudded across a sky that was fast changing from hazy blue to a threatening gray. The wide expanse of the river, placid just an hour earlier, was growing restless. Long, white-capped waves gathered speed and rolled toward the shore, breaking in sprays of watery foam.

To the east, where the great expanse of the sea stretched out to the horizon, heavy banks of fog began to gather as they moved landward. And from the fog, sailing along like the apparition of a dream, came a majestic schooner. It moved with a swiftness that lent unreality to the scene, its sails first blending with the fog, then billowing out to catch the wind.

The vessel seemed to grow in magnitude as it neared the island's shoreline. With a wide and graceful sweep, it approached so closely that the children gasped for breath at its beauty. As the schooner turned broadside, they could distinctly see two men on her starboard deck dragging what appeared to be a large sack. Bracing themselves against the rail, the sailors hoisted their burden over the edge and watched as it hit the water with a heavy splash. For a moment the sack seemed to bob about erratically as though it had some inner movement. And then as the rising waves engulfed it, the sack disappeared. Relieved of their burden, the sailors turned on their heels and walked away.

Still fascinated by the graceful movements of the schooner, the two girls watched as its sails luffed momentarily and then billowed out once more. Like a graceful seabird soaring on swift currents of air, the vessel keeled to port, reached for the wind, and then raced before it with a wall of white foam rippling along its hull. Their last sight of the ship was like a mirage—a shadow wavering in the distance only to be swallowed by a thick fog bank. The girls stood silently for a long, breathless moment, uncertain of what they had seen. Had it been a dream? An apparition conjured up by their exhaustion and the rising fog?

It was Angel who finally broke the silence. "I neber seen such!" she stammered. "Be I dreamin', Laura? Did you see um too?"

Laura May nodded without speaking.

"Like a bird—like a big, white bird comin' outta de fog."

"Whatcha think was in that sack they threw overboard, Angel?" Hesitating to consider what she had seen, Laura's eyes suddenly grew wide with excitement. "Hey, maybe it was a pirate ship! What if that sack was full of gold coins? Gilly's told me heaps of stories 'bout pirates. Use to be lots of 'em on these islands. Gilly said so. Oh, Angel, I bet that's just what they were."

"Mercy me! Don't want no pirates round hey're!" Angel's voice grew high with alarm. "Mayhap we bes' go home, Laura."

"Oh, fiddledeedee, don't be such a scaredy-cat. 'Sides, they're gone now. Come on, let's find Gilly and Zach. Wait till we tell 'em we saw a whole ship full of pirates." Picking up the trail once more, the girls continued on their way, but the going was rough, the land growing uneven and pockmarked with muddy depressions.

"Listen, Angel, we've got to get closer to the river. You'll never make it across all of this mud. Looks like there's a wide strip of sand down there that'll be easier to walk on."

Angel nodded, but her enthusiasm was waning. She desperately wanted to go back home. The sun had disappeared, and it was growing colder. Worse than that, she was feeling the beginnings of an unnamed fear as though something dangerous waited ahead of them. Laura, however, was obviously determined to find her brother. Moving on with a dogged determination, she now seemed oblivious to Angel's exhaustion.

Struggling across the remnants of an old dune, the children finally reached its crest and stopped to catch their breaths. Grasses and vines had overgrown the embankment, hiding the erosion beneath. Unsuspecting of the danger, Laura May grasped Angel's arm for balance and leaned forward to search for a way down. But she had no more turned her head than the sandy soil beneath her feet began to crumble and give way. Grasping wildly at her friend's arm, Laura felt herself sliding down the embankment. Angel tried to pull her back, but it was impossible. With a cry of fear, she, too, lost her balance and tumbled head over heels through a blinding landslide of loose sand and flailing grasses.

Their fall was broken by a pile of dried salt hay that lay like a ragged wall along the high tide line. The water-soaked shafts of cord grass smelled strongly of the sea, an odor that when carried by a fresh wind is bracing and pleasant. But any pleasantries that the hay might have had were entirely erased by the overpowering smell of dead sea life. Bits of dried seaweed and shell creatures had been trapped in the salt hay. Left to lie in the sun, their odor had become nothing short of nauseating. Not more than a foot to their left was the rotting remains of a huge horseshoe crab. It lay upside down, its claws sprawled in grotesque disarray.

To make matters worse, the girls' sudden descent had disturbed a cloud of stinging flies. Angered by the intruders, the flies swarmed upward and then zeroed in for the attack. Desperately seeking escape from the offensive straw, Laura pulled herself to her hands and knees and clawed her way toward the open strip of sand.

Angel tried to follow, but her awkward legs would not let her move with the same speed. Having dropped her crutches in the fall, she lay stunned and disoriented. "Laura—Laura May—he'p we!"

"Angel, grab my hand. Come on—reach for me!"

"Mah crutches! I dun lost mah crutches!"

"Don't cry. We'll find them. Reach for my hand, and I'll pull you out."

Wading chest high into the pile of cord grass, Laura grabbed for her friend's outstretched hand and tried to pull. But Angel's hands were wet from the water-logged hay. With a screech of fright, the black child fell backward again, this time wrenching her weak ankles as she fell. It took several more tries before she finally lay wet and sobbing on the sand of the riverbank.

"Angel, I'm sorry. I didn't know that would happen. Here, maybe if we press up close to each other, it won't be so cold."

Angel was trembling so hard that her teeth clicked together. Her legs felt numb, and her twisted feet and ankles were starting to swell. Miraculously, Laura had come out unscathed, but her woolen frock was damp and cold. It wasn't long before her teeth began to chatter too. Trying to borrow warmth from each other, they huddled together and surveyed the dark water of the river.

Overhead, angered by the intruders on their stretch of beach, a raucous flock of gulls flew about haphazardly. Then spotting a school of silvery fish darting through the waves, the gulls forgot the cause of their anger and went into action. Gaining altitude, they swirled over the girls' heads, and then one by one began to dive toward the breaking surf.

Trying to escape this onslaught of predators from the sky, the tiny fish hurtled themselves through the crests of the breaking waves until the water's surface fairly boiled with their flying, silvery bodies. The gulls caught them in midair, screaming in triumph as they ascended with the hapless fish dangling from their bills. Some gulls, lazier than the others, made no effort to dive into the waves after the racing fish, choosing instead to steal from those who had done all the work.

"How can those silly gulls scream so loud when their mouths are full?" wondered Laura in dismay. "Look at 'em. What a pack of thieves! They're snatching food right from each other's beaks! Maum Beezie'd have our hides if we tried . . ." Laura's voice trailed off into silence as she looked down at the face of her friend.

Angel sat rigidly staring at the river, her mouth wide with shock and her dark eyes filled with horror. "Laura . . ." Her voice cracked and broke. "Laura . . . you . . . you see what I see?" Lifting a trembling hand, she pointed at the incoming waves.

Laura spun around, dropped her lower jaw in dismay, and then sank to her knees. She felt a cold tremor of fear and revulsion move through her. A large object was floating in the water not more than a hundred feet from where they sat. With each receding wave, dark water eddied around it, leaving slow-spreading circles moving shoreward. Another wave began to build and move toward the floating mass. Something long and tentaclelike lifted up, wavered as though to fend off the pounding wall of water, and then dropped back with a splash. Hungry for its prey, the wave hit, swirling over the flotsam, sucking it under in a whirlpool of dark water and white foam.

The girls stood transfixed. It was like watching a monstrous cat playing with its defenseless victim. Again and again the object resurfaced, only to be sucked back into the pounding surf. Then a wave larger than its fellows caught at the mass and lifted it high onto the crest. With a sound like the crack of a whip, the wave curled and broke into splinters of flashing water and foam. The sack of flotsam was thrown toward the shore as though it was nothing more than a useless clump of seaweed.

Both Laura and Angel let out a piercing cry of alarm when the sacklike object hit the wet sand of the beach. For several moments there was no movement to it. Then with a sudden spasm, it seemed to arch upward and belch out a great puddle of water.

Moving forward, the girls were almost upon it when the watersoaked sack arched again, let out a hiss of air, and then rolled over to reveal the ashen face of a man. The girls stopped in midstep, too overcome with shock to move closer. The man tried to lift his arm again, as though he were still fighting the waves, but the exertion was too much. With a final tremor the arm collapsed and fell limply across the man's chest while a pool of dark water formed under his body. His eyes stared sightlessly at the lowering sky. His mouth hung open as though a cry for mercy had died on his lips.

Still hungry for its lost prey, the river licked at the remains, then receded once more, leaving a trail of dirty foam on the hard-packed sand. The man lay still. Only the cry of the gulls and the gurgling surf disturbed the silence of the beach. Trying to summon up her courage, Laura moved tentatively toward the man. He was limp, legs spread-eagled, one arm twisted beneath him, the other lying across his chest. Remnants of clothing hung in wet tatters from his shriveled body. His kinky hair, encrusted as it was with crystals of salt, glistened in the waning light. He was obviously a Negro, but the color of his skin had lost its smooth blackness, replaced by a sickly gray sheen.

Angel moved up close and grasped Laura's arm for support, but there was no support to be had. Their legs gave way simultaneously. Slumping to the cold sand, the children could do nothing but hold each other tight and wait for deliverance.

Laura May Weldon had just turned seven. Though young, she

was already in command of her world. Born into the privileged society of the Low Country planter, she could lay claim to both wealth and status. And while affluence is not always the forerunner of leadership, in Laura's case there was an abundance of both. Adults deferred to her wishes, not because they were commanded to do so, but simply because she gave them that desire. She possessed a large helping of determination tempered by a caring personality, all of which made her a joy to be with.

Laura May's admiring followers began with the Negro child who now clung to her in stunned silence. Angel was also seven, and like Laura she had been born on the Weldon Plantation. In all else, however, the two girls were as different as the river from the sea. Angel lacked both wealth and privilege. She had never known her father; her mother had died giving her birth. While Laura was healthy and strong, Angel struggled through life on painfully twisted feet.

But of all the afflictions that Angel bore, none was so burdensome as the color of her skin. Condemned to a life of servitude by virtue of her pigmentation, she could claim nothing as her own, not even her body. Born a slave, descended from a long line of slaves, Angel's prospects of one day outreaching her lowly status seemed virtually nil. But like the water of the river's channel, Angel's thoughts ran deep. She had a quick mind and a ravenous thirst for knowledge. Nothing escaped her. She absorbed information like the marsh absorbs the incoming tide.

With such differences it would hardly seem possible for a friendship to flower. Nevertheless, Laura May and Angel were inseparable. Such friendships were not uncommon on the southern plantations of the 1800s. Indeed, with slaves outnumbering planters a hundred to one, a planter's children seldom had a choice in the matter of playmates.

It was not lack of choice, however, that drew Laura and Angel together. The very circumstances of their births connected their lives. Maum Beezie's midwifery skills had helped them both come into the world. And now it was her unselfish love that served to fuse their friendship.

For seven years Maum Beezie had been the center of the universe for the two children. Sitting in her old rocking chair by the nursery-room hearth, she would cuddle them close and sing the old songs of faith and courage, her Gullah dialect coming soft and sweet:

De ol' sheep done kno' de road.
De ol' sheep done kno' de road.
De ol' sheep done kno' de road.
De young lambs mus' fin' de way.

"Hear we sing'n, chilluns?" she'd say, a smile creasing her shiny black face. "Now le'see effen de young lambs what's settin' hey're in Maum Beezie's lap kin sing lika dem angels ob heaben."

Clapping their hands in time with the words, the two children would join in on the chorus:

Shout, my brotha, you are free!
De young lambs mus' fin' de way
Christ has brought you liberty!
De young lambs mus' fin' de way.*

Then they would laugh together while Maum Beezie's musical voice went on into another song or a story or maybe just a quiet hum.

And there were other things she taught them: values that would get them through the rough spots in life. Things like hope and loyalty. Angel hadn't yet reached the age where she needed to understand hope, but for a child born into slavery, loyalty was almost second nature.

Laura had her share of loyalty, although it came out in a different way. Instinctively knowing her black companion's physical limitations, she was always ready to lend a hand, taking upon herself both the role of guardian and defender. The foolhardy person who thought to take advantage of Angel's deformities was certain to find himself facing the brunt of Laura's wrath.

But nothing could have prepared them for this! Coming face to face with cruelty and intolerance, the children had only each other to cling to.

It was almost dark when the search party found the girls. They were sitting huddled together on the beach, arms folded across their chests, their heads resting on each other's shoulders. Though they had fallen asleep, their faces were not those of small children at peace; they appeared haggard and sunken, as though what they had seen had aged them in an instant. Laura May whimpered when her father lifted her into his arms and pressed her against his chest, but she didn't open her eyes.

Gilly and Zach were with the search party, having been on their way home when they met the men at the edge of the marsh. Zach reached down for Angel and felt the coldness of her frail little body. He rubbed her legs and her twisted feet, trying to bring warmth back to them. Finally, he pulled off his own coat and wrapped her in it, then lifted her up and cradled her close to his body.

Gullah Jim, the plantation's elderly fisherman, had been the first to spot the girls. None too soon either. The sky was growing black with night and building storm clouds. Cruising along the riverbank, he had feared the children had been playing too close to the water. If that were the case, they could easily have been swept out with the tide. He instinctively knew that in such a case they might never be found. But worse than that, the thought that gnawed most at his innards was that he might find their small bodies washed up on shore.

When he spotted the sacklike object in the dim light, his heart lurched in his chest, and his mouth went dry as cotton. Was it one of them—or maybe both wrapped up together in death? Poling his bateau in for a closer look, his attention was drawn to the small, huddled lump near the sack. There was no movement there either, at least none that he could see. But something told him there was life to it.

Sliding his craft smack into a sandbar, he jumped out without remembering to anchor it down. He could see the body of the man clearly now. Obviously dead. The little huddle was the children. The slow rise and fall of their chests filled him with relief. Without hesitation he ran back to his boat and pulled out the old Brown Bess rifle the master had given him.

Two shots in the air. Three. Men's voices came down through the marsh. A shout, and the whole search team was running, coming toward the beach en masse, torches quivering through the darkness. Shouting back and forth—relief in the voices. They had found the children—alive!

"Poor devil! Never stood a chance," someone commented.

Gilly leaned over the man's body and prodded it with the toe of his boot. "Look's mighty shrunken, doesn't he? S'pose the water's done that?"

Gullah Jim ran his hand over the man's chest, lifting the limp arms so he could see the skin beneath. The glistening white remnants of old welts were visible on the sides of the rib cage. "Poor devil!" Jim said again, this time with anger at the edge of his voice. "Done had a few too many licks ob de lash. Half-starved too."

Gilly squatted down to take a closer look. "But where did he come from? I've never seen him before—not on any of the places here abouts."

"Mm-mm, not from hey're bouts, Massa Gilly. Come offa dat ship."

"Ship? What ship?"

"Dat slaber what come flyin' low into de bay like she tryin' ta outrun de patrol boats."

"Slaver? You mean a contraband slave ship?"

"Um-hm, dat what I mean." Jim's voice was low, his teeth clenched in an anger that was just short of rage. "Come in like de angel ob death heself. Throw off de cargo what's too rotten ta sell."

Gilly shivered and stood up. Stepping back from the body, he tried to regain control, but his stomach was lurching, and bile was rising in his mouth.

A third man walked up to them, a young Negro with a lean frame and a fine-chiseled face. He would have been strikingly handsome if it weren't for the two white scars that ran across his right cheek. His bearing was just short of noble, lessened only by the haughty look of pride that pulled his mouth into a sneer.

"Not a pretty sight, is it, buckra boy!"

"Watch you mouf, Cudjo!" Jim jumped up and stepped close to the young black man. "Massa he'e you talkin' lik-a dat, you find yo'self in somebody else's cotton field—one you gotta hoe 'stead ob jes lookin' at."

Cudjo pushed the old fisherman away with contempt. "When I need your advice, old man, I'll ask. Till then, you keep your distance."

"Stop it!" shouted Gilly. "Stop it—both of you! We've got to get this poor fellow's body back to the grounds. The least we can do is give him a decent Christian burial."

Cudjo slapped his thigh and let out a shout of laughter. "Decent Christian burial! Who you talkin' about, boy? This daid nigger ain't no Christian. They brought him straight from Africa. Best you leave him to Cudjo. He know how to bury an African."

"Poor devil!" muttered Gilly. Bowing his head into the wind, he followed the waving torches of the search party back along the dark beach toward the grounds of the Big House.

---

* Ronald Daise, *Reminiscences of a Sea Island Heritage* (Orangeburg, S.C.: Sandlapper, 1986), p. 36.

2
Roll, Jordan, Roll

(1858)

Cepin de Lawd make de house, de wok ob dem wa make um ain't mount ta notin (Psalm 127:1).

As they approached the dock of their Coosaw Island plantation, the lead boatman shouted into the distance and flashed the lantern as a signal. There was a long silence, answered finally by an echoing call. Flecks of light sputtered and then flared up as the fire of the shoreline torches caught hold. Gilly sighed with relief, thankful that his ordeal was nearly over. Since their last angry outburst in Beaufort, he and his father had hardly spoken a civil word to each other.

It was spring on the Sea Islands, and on any other such evening, Gilly would have enjoyed the river journey home from Beaufort. A humid listlessness clung to the air, foretelling the approach of summer. Polliwogs and minnows swarmed in the shallows, while wisteria and trumpet vines heavy with blossoms swayed from the tops of the tallest pines. A flock of white egrets swooped silently down through the rising mist, and like the large, wet flakes of a late snowfall settled upon the filigreed branches of an ancient cypress.

Sitting at the stern of the flat-bottomed boat, Gilly stared sullenly into the dark water. Both river and sky mirrored his mood. Having gorged itself with the incoming tide, the wide estuary that ran from the sea toward the inland islands lay listless and silent. The day was fast fading, leaving the western horizon piled high with purple clouds so thick that the last rays of sunshine could barely penetrate them. Was this the ominous peace before a storm, he wondered, or was it simply an illusion caused by his own growing depression? But the beauty of the river was still there. Perhaps if he concentrated on it, he would find some last shreds of happiness within its depths.

Pulling hard against the poles of their long oars, the Negro boatmen stroked to the beat of "Roll, Jordan, Roll," a much-loved spiritual. Their voices were deep with expression and yearning, their bodies swaying hypnotically with the rhythm.

Gilly could see his father sitting on a coil of rope in the prow, his body slumped, his chin resting on his chest and a low, rumbling snore coming from his half-opened mouth. Flickering lantern light illuminated Gilbert Weldon's features but did little to soften the stern lines of his face. It was as though the man had spent so many years practicing firmness that even in his sleep he could not relax.

Tipping his head slightly, Gilly studied his father's face. What had happened to this man whom he had once tried so hard to please? That was long ago. There was no pleasing him now, not for Gilly. Only Laura May could do that. She had him twisted around her fingers, playing to his every whim, cajoling smiles from him when no one else could.

No matter. She was just a child. Let her get what enjoyment she could out of life while it was still hers to be had. The dreams of childhood fade soon enough. Of greater concern to Gilly was his father's apparent blindness to the political changes going on around him. Did the man really fail to see what was coming, or had he simply chosen to ignore it? Gilly's greatest fear was that his father's economic success had so warped his thinking that he could no longer distinguish between good and evil. In which case, considering the rumblings of unrest that were even now sweeping the South, Gilly could not help but wonder if his own future was in serious jeopardy.

Gilly could sense the approach of disaster, could even smell and taste it. The South's plantation society was slowly but surely disintegrating. It was a fading dream in which a chosen few preened the soft, white feathers of their own greed while a thousand overworked blacks beat back the flames of doom.

The South's talk of secession from the Union, which had started more than fifty years ago, was growing stronger every day. In fact, it was now only a matter of time. And of all the southern states, it was South Carolina that carried the lead in this most drastic of remedies to the mounting list of political, social, and economic problems. No wonder this trip home felt like a funeral procession!

Rubbing his hands together, Gilly tried to ease the feeling of numbness. The joints of his fingers ached with tension; even the muscles of his jaw felt frozen. The lines of anger had stretched down the corners of his mouth and pulled his cheeks into hard, diagonal ridges.

Perhaps he was partly to blame for this latest argument. He should have kept his mouth closed, held in his feelings. But he had had no choice; his father, with typical insensitivity, had pushed things over the edge. Yes, it was his father who must take the lion's share of the blame for the rift that now lay between them. And this time, Gilly pounded his fist against the railing as they approached the dock, this time he wasn't going to give in! Let the old man rant and rave. This time he would stand up for his rights. He looked once more at his father and then turned his back in disgust.

Gilbert Weldon had become alert as soon as they'd rounded the last bend. He stood with his legs spread wide and his hips braced against the rail; the look on his face was as hard and unyielding as that of his son's. He had an urge to pound his fists together and shout his frustration into the darkness. But no, he must restrain himself. It wouldn't do to have his darkies see any loss of control. He prided himself on that. Other masters might let their anger fly in acts of uncontrolled rage. Not Gilbert Weldon.

But blast the boy! Why must he always act the traitor? What kind of a man would he be if now, under the pressures of a few political changes, he couldn't stand on principle? The problem was, he didn't know when he was well off. He had been given too much, been too pampered and coddled. Gilbert felt a surge of apprehension. Whose fault was that? Was it his? Had he failed as a father? Gone were his dreams of slipping into a peaceful retirement while his son took over the cultivation of some of the richest cotton land in the South. Gone, too, was the camaraderie that should have accompanied a father and son on what he had hoped would be an adventure into manhood.

Having spent three days in Beaufort, one of which entailed a four-hour session with his attorney, Master Weldon was now more than ready to return to the peace and solitude of his island plantation. Only it wasn't entirely his now. Thinking that responsibility was the key to maturity, he had had the papers drawn up to make his son a full partner and half-owner of Weldon Oaks. What a fool he'd been to move so quickly! Obviously, Gilly lacked the common sense the good Lord had given him. Nor did he seem to have the ability to appreciate the magnitude of what he had been so freely given.

Gilbert scratched his well-trimmed beard and spat at the dark shadow of a catfish circling in the reflected torchlight. Perhaps he should have talked to the boy first, told him what he'd been planning. But the whole thing was supposed to be a surprise, a birthday gift, of sorts. He'd thought for certain the lad would be more than thrilled with the arrangements. How many sixteen-year-olds get half of their inheritance before their father is even dead! Besides, it was the intelligent thing to do: hands-on training with an experienced elder there to advise and encourage.

The trip into town had started out badly. First, there was that unfortunate drowning before they left home. Gilly had gotten himself all worked up over that. Gilbert Weldon shook his head sadly. No doubt about it, the boy would have to harden himself to such things; they were simply a part of the life into which he had been born.

Then upon reaching Beaufort they had found the place all abuzz with political talk about impending secession. Gilbert was out and out for it and didn't hesitate to give his son his considered opinion on the subject. He was thoroughly convinced that despite its lack of industry, the South simply had to insulate itself from the repressive tactics of the northern states. Northern politicians had no understanding of the South's agrarian society with its dependence on slave labor, nor were they ready to grant southern states the freedom to regulate their own domestic policies. But Gilly, having picked up some euphoric notions about nationalism, was incensed by his father's political views. Their discussion had very quickly turned into an overheated argument.

Under the circumstances, perhaps Gilly's reaction to having some of the plantation's burdens shifted onto his own shoulders was understandable. But the sheer force of the boy's escalating anger had left Gilbert shocked almost beyond words. Closing his eyes, he relived the argument he had had with his son blow by blow.

"You're giving me a full partnership?" Gilly had asked, surprise lacing the edges of his voice. They were standing in the parlor of their Beaufort house, a stately mansion that faced the wide expanse of the river with its bordering fringes of marsh grass. The tide was slowly ebbing, exposing the mud flats and their bristling coat of oyster beds.

Standing with his arms akimbo, his head cocked to one side, Gilly looked at his father questioningly. "Why now? I've barely turned sixteen, and there's a major political crisis brewing right under our noses. Isn't your action a bit premature? Surely you're joking, Father."

"Joking? Why should I joke about such a matter. What does secession have to do with Weldon Oaks? The plantation needs to keep running, doesn't it? The rise or fall of the Union doesn't alter that."

For an answer, Gilly simply slapped the heel of his hand against his forehead and turned his back on his father.

"Listen, son, the day is coming when you'll thank me for this move . . ."

Gilly spun around, his voice strident and his face contorted with frustrated anger. The muscles of his neck stood out like cords, and his hands were clenched into tight fists. "*I don't want it!* I don't want either the plantation or its slaves."

Gilbert was stunned into silence. Why, the boy acted as though the place was nothing more than a clapboard shack and a collection of weed fields! Whatever had gotten into him?

"Father, putting politics aside, there's more to this, and you know it. Why won't you even try to understand? We've been skirting around this issue for months. It's time we faced it square on. The fact is, secession or no secession, I don't want to spend the rest of my life on an isolated island raising cotton! It's a dirty business from top to bottom. Day after day, I've watched you bully those poor, overworked field hands. And what do they get out of it? Their only reward is a crumbling hovel to live in and a muddy grave by the river as their final resting place!"

"What are you talking about!" shouted Gilbert. "You know perfectly well that I take good care of my people. They want for . . ."

"*Your* people? Oh, yes, Father, that's always the way it is— *your* people, working *your* acres, living on *your* generosity. Don't you see? Why, to hear you talk, one would think you were some kind of deity. Actually, I find that repulsive. I'm not like you. I never will be like you. And try as you might, Father, you are *not* a god! You can't re-create me in your own image."

Gilbert had sucked in his breath so hard he'd felt something snap in the muscles of his rib cage. "What are you talking about, boy? Have you been reading that fool trash those northern abolitionists have been spreading around? Why, you miserable ingrate! So you think raising cotton and making a few field hands do a decent day's work is a dirty business, do you? Well, I'd like you to know it's put food in your belly and clothes on your back for these past sixteen years!

"And as for *my people*"—Gilbert pressed the tip of his index finger into his son's chest—"don't you ever forget that that's exactly what they are, *my people*. If it weren't for me, it is highly doubtful that a tenth of them would survive. They simply don't have the mental capacity to do so. They're nothing but children— ignorant children who need direction and discipline." Gilbert had warmed to his subject now. This was an argument he had long ago won with himself. He had all the answers down pat. Stomping back and forth across the floor, his voice rose in righteous indignation. "Do you think those poor niggers would have had it any better back in Africa? Hardly! They've been selling each other off into slavery for generations. If they weren't slaves to white men, they'd be slaves to each other. And they've been digging in the dirt for generations. They lived in mud huts and spent more time starving than they ever did filling their bellies."

Turning to face his son head on, Gilbert pressed his argument home. "I never laid a whip on one of 'em in my entire life. I never starved 'em, nor let 'em go cold in the winter. They have decent roofs over their heads and clothes on their backs. They don't have to worry about taxes or bill collectors, nor sit up half the night trying to balance books that—"

Gilly jumped to his feet. "I know! I know! I've heard all of this a hundred times over." His voice rose above the clatter of wagon wheels in the street below. Pressing his face close to his father's, Gilly dropped his tone, but the accusation of his words bit as hard as the teeth of a steel trap. "Nor have you ever given them the freedom to *try* to live without your magnanimous support. If they're ignorant children, it's because you've kept them that way for your own greedy purposes. Has it ever entered your mind that more than just a few of them might actually be a heap smarter than you are?"

Stopping to catch his breath, Gilly turned back toward the window. He tried to calm himself. The window was wide open to let in the spring breeze. Out on the street, a small group of curious passersby were glancing surreptitiously at the house. Seeing him standing there, they dropped their heads and scurried on. Only an old Negro man who was hawking fish and shrimp from a small pushcart remained. The air around the cart was thick with flies. Picking up a palm frond, the old man fanned them away. Then, with a worried glance at the window, he, too, hurried on.

Gilly took a deep breath. How could his father be such a fool? Turning once more to face him, Gilly was struck anew by the stupidity of the man's argument. "Maybe that's what scares you—the fact that if given half the chance, they may well have enough intelligence to get the better of you. Maybe that's why you and the entire South, for that matter, try so hard to keep them ignorant. Passing laws to make it a capital offense to teach a Negro to read and write is unconscionable!"

Clenching his fists in anger, Gilly walked back to his father and faced him head on. "But that's not enough for you, is it? You control the lives and destinies of more than a hundred Negroes, and now you intend to do the same thing with your own son. You're just itching to plan every step of my life. Well, I don't want your indentured servitude, Father! I want to be my own person, choose my own life, fulfill my own destiny!"

Rage rose in Gilbert like an unchecked fever. He had to get control of himself, or he'd have an attack of apoplexy. His hands tightened at his sides; it was all he could do to resist balling them into fists and striking Gilly full in the face. Spinning around on his heels, he slammed his fist instead into the small end table sitting next to his favorite armchair. A porcelain figurine that had been sitting on the table clattered to the floor and broke into a hundred pieces.

"Get ahold of yourself, Gilbert," he said under his breath. After all, the boy *is* still young. He doesn't understand. He needs a few more years under his belt to see how hard this world really is. Turning to face his son once more, Gilbert resolved to say something conciliatory. But Gilly's expression, the smirk of defiance on his lips and the cold steeliness of his eyes, wiped away all thoughts of a truce. He couldn't resist inflicting one final jab. "All right, boy, suppose you tell me exactly what it is you plan on doing for a living when you finally get around to growing up?"

Gilly wiped the perspiration from his brow and pulled away from his father. His voice softened. "I—I'm sorry, Father. I didn't mean to upset you. But can't you see, I'm just not cut out to be a planter. I've given a lot of thought as to what I'd really like to do with my life and . . ."

"Well, spit it out! What brilliant plans have you hatched up?" Gilbert didn't like this new turn of events. Perhaps the boy was right. Perhaps he'd been a little heavy-handed at times. But Gilly was immature in his thinking; he wasn't ready to start making decisions on his own just yet. That was the whole purpose of this partnership: to teach him how to think things out, train him in the ways of . . .

"I—I'd like to go to sea, Father. I'd like to . . ."

"*What! To SEA*? You mean to tell me you want to spend the rest of your life floating around on some stinking scow? You want to grow old and bent pulling in nets and cleaning fish? Is that what you call 'clean' work?"

"No—no, sir. Not that at all. I wasn't thinking of fishing. I'd like to go to the new naval academy in Annapolis—learn to be a first-rate seaman."

"*Never*!" Gilbert smashed his fist into the table once again, this time hitting it with such force that it broke in two and fell to the floor with a resounding crash. "No son of mine is going to become a common deckhand! Go to sea, indeed! Have you lost your mind?"

"Father, didn't you hear a word I said? I don't want to become a common sailor. I said that I want to go to the naval academy—become a naval officer."

"You'll go to the devil first! Get out of my way, boy. I've had as much of you as I can stomach for one day!"

And with that, Gilbert Weldon had stormed out of their Beaufort house. He did not come back that night. When he finally did return the next morning, just an hour before having to catch the tide back to Coosaw, there was the smell of stale whisky on his breath. His eyes were bloodshot, his clothes disheveled, and his mouth was clamped in a tight, unyielding line.

Now with the flatbed moving at a slow pace toward the half-finished dock, the tension in the air was still as heavy as a bale of water-soaked cotton. Both father and son were anxious to get to shore. The boat wasn't big enough for the two of them. They needed room; wide-open spaces to avoid each other. Even their most casual glances were lethal—as though eye contact was all that was needed to spring the deadly trap of words that lay coiled, waiting to resurface. Resentment crouched in every corner of the boat, its eyes steel hard with betrayal.

Even Zach could feel the tension in the air. He had slept fitfully most of the way home curled up on a sack of grain just a few feet from his young master. Having been away from the house on an errand, he didn't know the nature of the bone these two men who owned him were picking at. He felt certain, however, that it was something that would ultimately change their relationship and perhaps his own precarious standing.

Finally the boat bumped against the pilings of the dock, and Master Weldon jumped off, barking orders to crew and waiting docksmen alike. Zach got up the courage to approach Gilly. "Ma-

massa Gilly," he stammered, "why fer you face draggin' pon de deck all de way home?"

Gilly turned to him with agitation in his eyes. "When are you going to learn to stop calling me 'massa'? Haven't I asked you a thousand times not to?"

"Yes'su, sho nuff you hab. But dere stands you pappy lookin' like he gwanna freeze ober de gates ob hell, and dis po' niggra ain't gwanna oil de hinges right in front ob he!"

Gilly smiled crookedly. He and Zach, despite their differences in status, had always been the closest of friends. That was the one right thing his father had done for him, giving him Zach as his "daily give servant." It had happened when the two of them were about the same age as Laura May and Angel were now. And like the two little girls, the relationship had never been that of master and slave. Gilly suspected that his father understood. After all, didn't the plantation's master have the same sort of relationship with Gullah Jim, the elderly black fisherman?

Pulling the black boy aside, Gilly decided that if he was going to confide in anyone, it would be Zach. "Listen, Zach, I've decided that I've taken all I can from my father. He won't even consider that I might have my own dreams, my own plans for the future."

Zach nodded, but said nothing.

"Do you know what this trip to Beaufort was really all about?" Gilly asked, keeping his voice low so that no one but Zach would hear.

Zach shook his head.

"My father has come up with a scheme to entrap me—to keep me here on this stinking island until I'm an old man and as warped in my thinking as he is. Not a word of warning did he give me, not even a hint as to the real nature of this trip."

Gilly looked deeply into Zach's eyes, willing him to understand the nature of his predicament. " 'A few days in town,' Papa said. 'Do you a world of good. Get away from the womenfolk with all their hand wringing and long faces.' Can you believe it? Can you believe the man could be that shallow?"

"What you mean, Gilly? Why for he be shallow jes 'cause he say he gwanna take you ta Beaufort?"

"A man just drowned right here on our property! Of course the women were upset. So was everyone else, with the one exception of my beloved father! No, that didn't bother him one bit. 'Just a slave,' he said. 'Nothing to get riled over.' I tell you, Zach, the man doesn't have a sympathetic bone in his body! And that's what he wants me to become: a hardened, callow fool! Why, he honestly thinks the world ought to revolve around him!"

"Now, Gilly, don't unrable you mouf' lik-a-dat. You pappy, he a strong mouf', but he don't always mean what he say. Course de drownin' ob dat po' ol' niggra wex he. Why for you t'ink he rush off ta Beaufort lik-a-dat?"

Gilly looked at Zach incredulously. "Why are you of all people defending him? Do you enjoy being a slave—being treated like one of his oxen or mules? Do you know what he said when I suggested that we should at least wait until the man was buried? 'Let the slaves bury their own,' that's what he said. 'I've got better things to do than sit in on the funeral of every nigger who washes up onto the beach.' Well, does that tell you anything about what kind of a dear, old master my father is?"

Zach stepped backward, afraid to show even Gilly the true nature of his feelings. Loyalty to the master had been inbred in him, but deep down inside he seethed with burning resentment. If Gilly unearthed it now, tried to dig it up with the venom of his own dissatisfaction, there was no telling how it might explode.

"*Zach!*" Master Weldon's stern voice nipped off the fuse of his anger like the crack of a whip. "Get your black hide over here and help with the unloading. Since when are you privileged enough to stand around like a prima donna while everyone else does the work?"

Watching from the shadows, Gilly twisted his mouth into a sneer. "So much for me being his 'equal partner,'" he said under his breath. "He's still the Great White Master!"

3

All My Troubles, Lawd

(1858)

Fa sho, eby posin bon gwine habe trouble, sho as de spaak fly op from de fiah (Job 5:7).

The small line of boatmen moved slowly up the darkened lawn toward the Big House, each man balancing on his head some of the provisions purchased in Beaufort by Master Weldon just the day before. Having planned for his family's migration back to their Beaufort home before the start of the "sickly season," the master was now stocking up for those who would remain behind on the island. This included virtually all of the field and yard hands; indeed, most of them never left the island at all.

Despite a high mortality rate, the planters considered their slaves immune to the sicknesses that swept through the outer islands during the summer months. Only a few carefully chosen servants accompanied the family on its yearly sojourn into town.

The church graveyard gave ample credence to Gilbert Weldon's fears. Deaths from malaria, yellow fever, or encephalitis were all too common, and plantation owners had a meager choice of medicines to fight off the dread specter of disease. Life for those who survived wasn't anything to be envied either. Left with the debilitating effects of recurring fevers and exhaustion, the sufferers often found that their ultimate fate was still an early grave.

Beginning in late spring, when the steamy marshes gave off a vapor of fetid air during the day, often turning into a thick fog by night, the danger period extended well into the fall, when the first frost nipped at the tips of the marsh grasses. The sluggish rivers, low marshlands, and stagnant swamps of summer were the breeding places for all manner of diseases, chief among which was the dreaded scourge of malaria.

Gilbert Weldon felt a real concern for his family on this matter and made it a point to move them into town well before a hint of the miasma began. As a reminder, he had attached to the inside cover of his journal an article that had been clipped from a State Agricultural Society pamphlet. The clipping contained an excerpt from an "Essay on Malaria" presented by Dr. S. H. Dickenson to the society's 1843 convention. Having researched the problem in some detail, the learned doctor had outlined what he and his colleagues believed to be both the nature and cause of the dread disease:

The beautiful and fertile low country of our State is the seat of annual and endemic visitations of disease, which we are accustomed to attribute to Malaria. Whatever may be the difference of opinion elsewhere as to the source of origin of the aerial poison, the Medical profession here is unanimous in regarding it as the result of vegetable decomposition in moist places at high temperatures.[1]

If Master Weldon surmised that Doctor Dickenson had rightly named the breeding grounds, but was well off the mark when it came to the transmission of the disease, it remained doubtful that he would have altered his custom. Being a man of habit, it would take nothing short of a major catastrophe to change his lifestyle. Little did he know, however, that on this eve of his return to Coosaw, catastrophe was already brewing. Not even the recent altercation with his son could have prepared him for the chain of events about to be visited upon his household.

Moving slowly up the gradual slope of the dirt roadway, the returning party seemed oblivious to the odd silence that met them. The river journey had been long, and the boatmen were bone weary from pulling on the oars. Now as they labored silently under their heavy loads, even the minimal sound of their bare feet striking the ground was obliterated by the soft sand of the roadway.

From this river approach, the Big House was well hidden behind a double row of live oaks, which lined either side of the road. Only the dock hand whose job it was to watch for the flatbed's return had greeted the master and his party. With his head held down respectfully, the dock hand simply mumbled a few words into the tattered collar of his shirt and then slipped silently back into the shadows.

As usual, the master took the lead. Gilbert felt exceptionally weary tonight; the strain of this trip had taken its toll. It was as though a heavy weight was pressing against his chest, making his breathing labored and ragged. The distance along the tree-lined roadway, though relatively short, seemed endless. How good it would feel to take off his boots and stretch himself out in his easy chair! He sniffed the air absent-mindedly, wondering if Marian had a fire going in the hearth. There was a heavy smell of wood smoke in the air. Odd, such a warm night hardly called for a fire.

Stepping from under the canopy of gnarled branches with their ragged curtains of Spanish moss, Gilbert lifted his head and glanced at the darkened house. Even in the shadowy moonlight one could appreciate its solid lines. It was a well-built structure, perfectly square and rimmed on three sides with a double-decked piazza that lent grace to an otherwise stern exterior. A row of slim, white columns supported the weight of the upper deck. Between each column ran a carved railing, which on the lower deck was overrun with honeysuckle vines.

A third railing, smaller than the ones below, bordered the upper edges of the roof. In daylight, one could see the copper-plated roof panels between the narrow slats of the upper rail. Over the years the copper had oxidized to a light shade of green, an effect both easy on the eyes and appropriate to the verdant landscape.

Gilbert's gaze moved downward, taking in the front of the house. He could just make out the wide set of steps that led up to the entranceway. Large double doors with their high fan windows had been set into a solid white frame to match the white wooden siding covering the outer walls. Sighing with relief, the master pushed a graying shock of hair from his forehead and began to move toward the steps. Yes, this was the kind of house a man took pride in coming home to.

He had hardly walked more than six feet, however, before the thought struck him—drew him up short. Something wasn't right. That smell was not from a simple hearth fire. It permeated the air, obliterating all other odors. And there was an ominous strangeness to the place, as though an undefined danger lurked in the shadows. Was it just the smell of burned-out fire? No, it was more than that. The house was too dark, not a light in it anywhere. Only a small lantern flickered at the top of the piazza stairs, casting dancing shadows against the dimly lighted entrance way.

Wait! What was that noise? Why, one of the doors had been left open. Even as the master watched, a gust of wind coming off the river licked at the swinging door and banged it back against the wooden siding of the house with a dull thud. Shocked into alertness, Gilbert stepped back and grasped at his son's arm.

"Something's wrong! There's been a fire. And look at the house; it's like a tomb. One of the doors has been left open!"

Gilly, like his father, had been numbed by exhaustion and preoccupied with his own thoughts. He had noticed the strong smell but failed to associate it with danger. Now, however, he too sensed what had been missing when they stepped onto the planks of the dock. It was not just the house that was excessively quiet; the entire grounds were all but deserted. His father's sudden reaction sent an electric shock up his spine that stopped him dead in his tracks. His innards went watery with fear as he studied the strangely darkened house.

A slave uprising! It was the first thought that came into Gilly's mind. He wanted to drop everything and race up the steps to the house, but a dread of what he might find there kept him rooted to the spot. The sickening image of rape and murder swam before his eyes. But the lantern—why was it sitting at the top of the steps? Was it a warning? A signal?

"Hsst! Stay where you are!" The boatmen, oblivious to everything but their own fatigue, had reached the top of the slope by now. Gilbert motioned for them to lay down their burdens and remain quietly back in the shadows. Detecting danger, the boatmen shrank back, the whites of their eyes growing large and luminous with fear. Not knowing whether fight or flight would be expected of them, they crouched against the tree trunks like cornered animals.

Reaching into his breast coat pocket, Gilbert pulled out a small revolver and began moving stealthily toward the steps. Gilly started to follow his father, but was waved back. The master could feel the pulse of blood quickening in his temples; the long muscles of his extremities grew taut. Alert to the smallest change, he sensed rather than heard someone approaching through the darkened wood line to the left of the house. Spinning suddenly in that direction, Gilbert bent his knees and raised his arms to shoulder level, with his hands clasped around the pistol and his index fingers tensed against the trigger.

Then with the realization that his small hand gun would be of little use if there was more than one attacker, he pulled himself up tall, squared his shoulders, and called out to the moving shadow in the woods. "Not a step farther—you hear me? Identify yourself! If I must, I'll fire and ask questions later."

"Hold on, Massa! Dis be Samuel—jes Samuel. No needs ta get riled."

With all thoughts of his earlier anger gone, Gilly stepped forward and placed his hand on his father's shoulder. His knees felt weak with relief at hearing Samuel's voice. Whatever else might be wrong, Samuel could be trusted.

Samuel was large boned and big muscled. He could pick up a mature watermelon with one hand. His shoulders were as broad as the door frame of his cabin, and he had to duck his head in order to enter it. Gilly had once seen him pull a sledge from a ditch that a mule was unable to budge. And along with his brawn, Samuel had brainpower. His was not the kind that came from books; Samuel couldn't read the first lick of writing. But what he lacked in learning, he made up for with wit, practicality, and, as Gullah Jim put it, a memory as uncommon as a two-tailed dog.

Seeing Samuel walking from the woods with his long, ground-eating strides, Master Weldon dropped his arms to his sides and relaxed his stance. Just to be safe, however, he kept his hand on the trigger of the pistol and his alert senses trained toward the Big House. He didn't wait for Samuel to reach him before asking the all-consuming question: "Well, what's happening? Speak up, man!"

Samuel slowed his pace as he approached the master and lowered his head respectfully. "Bad goin's on, massa, suh. Sumpin' done ketched fiah en de kitchen house early dis mornin' 'bout day clean. Whole place ben gutted afore de first bucket ob water get dere!"

Master Weldon's face went rigid with anger. "I've told Josephine a thousand times to watch that cookstove fire!"

"Tain't Josephine's fault, Massa Weldon, suh. She and de kitchen he'p was jes comin' in de place when dat fiah start. Don't start in de cookstove, nohow—start on de outside near de chimbly."

Gilbert cursed under his breath. He had checked out that chimney just days ago. It certainly had looked safe enough at the time.

Gilly blew out his breath in shock. "Was anyone injured?"

"Yes, suh, Massa Gilly." Samuel turned his face toward Gilly but kept his eyes on the master. "Josephine's hands done been burn right bad. She try ta beat out dat fiah wid she broom. Onliest, de broom, um caught fiah too. Po' ol' Josephine, she jes won't let go ob dat broom. Keep banging away at de flames shoutin', 'Lawd, Lawd, sabe mah kitchen! How I gwanna cook fo' de massa effen I hain't got no kitchen?'"

Gilly glanced sideward at his father and saw the man's anger toward his colored cook melt away like a glass of ice left sitting in the hot sun. Leave it to Samuel to cover a bad situation with a soothing word.

"All right, that explains the smell of burning," said the master as he shoved the pistol back into his breast coat pocket. "Of course, it's a loss, but kitchens can easily be replaced. What I really want to know is, why is the house so dark? Where's the mistress—and Maum Beezie? Where's Laura May?"

Gilly felt a new surge of apprehension working its way through his stomach and chest. There was more to this than an accidental kitchen fire, if, in fact, it was an accident at all!

"De missus an' Maum Beezie, dey take de chilluns down to de qua'ters."

"The quarters? What in the blazes—"

"Massa Weldon, suh, dey figure dat be best. Sumpin' mighty pecul'ar goin' on. You' fambly es jes' fine, so don't wex yous'f none. De missus, she stayin' in Maum Beezie's place till y'all come home. She axt we to keep a look-see fer ya'll, and dat's jes what I was a settin' out ta do dis bery minute. I pit dat lantern on de pizza so's y'all could see de way up de steps."

"Thank you, Samuel, I appreciate your loyalty. But exactly what, besides that kitchen fire, has happened around here?"

"Well, suh, like I say, it all start wid dat fiah. Eberybody come up hey're from de qua'ters ta help put um out. Den, next t'ing we know, Mr. Ned come runnin' up puffin' an' shoutin' dat de cane fiel' ben flooded."

"What! My overseer? What was he doing in the cane field while my kitchen house burned to the ground? Why, with a blaze that close, the Big House could have caught fire!" Suddenly Gilbert's face changed. His eyes opened wide with a look of startled incomprehension. "Wait! Hold on here. Wha—what do you mean, my cane field was flooded?"

Samuel stepped back a pace, not knowing which question to answer first. "Mr. Ned, he heye de sounds ob drum beats comin' from de direction ob de cane field. Get eberybody up hey're ta fight dat fire, den he skeedadle down ta de fields. Reckon he lookin' ta see who been beatin' dat drum."

Even in the dim light Gilly could see the color drain from his father's face. Those few special acres were Gilbert Weldon's pride and joy. Unlike the majority of the Sea Island planters, Gilbert had a taste for experimentation. He had taken the financial risk of turning some of his prime cotton land over to the cultivation of sugar cane. And over the past two years those cane fields had become an obsession with him.

Long-staple cotton had been the primary crop on these outer islands ever since the indigo culture had disappeared after the Revolution. Its cultivation, restricted by climate and soil conditions to those small bits of land along the South Carolina and northernmost Georgia coastline, had quickly turned its planters into a small but wealthy aristocracy. Considered a luxury item for its long, silky fibers and its superior strength, Sea Island cotton commanded fabulous prices on the European market. But of even greater importance was the fact that this prized cotton could spin as much as 300 hanks to the pound, twice the number of short-staple cotton. Thus, a Sea Island planter could realize huge profits if he put every available acre into cultivating the favored crop.[2]

Considering this, it was nothing short of miraculous that Gilbert Weldon had chosen to experiment with crop diversification. He had been forced to build special dikes and irrigation ditches around the cane to protect it from the close proximity to the ocean. High tides and coastal flooding were a constant worry. He had even taken some of his best hands from the cotton fields during the harvest season and set them to cutting cane.

If some considered this madness on his part, so be it. He took a devil-may-care pride in his adventurous spirit and spent long hours recording in minute detail every step of this, as a neighbor once labeled it, his "eccentric" research. So it was that Samuel's revelation caught Gilbert completely by surprise. Surely no one would be fool enough to tamper with his cane fields! "All right, Samuel, get to the point," the master demanded through clenched teeth. "Exactly *what* has happened to my cane fields?"

"It be de dikes, Massa Weldon, dey—well, suh, seems like dey broke jes when de tide come ta de flood."

"Impossible! New dikes don't just break, not by themselves. And the tide wasn't surging hard enough to break through. Something else—or somebody—must have broken them!"

"Yes, suh. I reckon dat's de trut'."

Gilbert spun around with such force that he nearly knocked Gilly down. "Boy, I want you to go down to the quarters and see to your mother and sister. Get them back to the house as fast as you can and see that they're comfortable."

Turning once more, Gilbert faced Samuel with angry determination. His words came out in short, crisp questions that stiffened the black man's body with alarm. "How bad are the breaks? How many hands does Ned have with him?"

"Mr. Ned got 'bout twenty hands wid him right now, suh. Been workin' all day, an' now dey es still out dere—workin' by lantern light. From de marks on what's left ta de dikes, well, suh, look like de water came up um 'bout high as mah knees."

"That's more than a foot high!" gasped the master. "The field would be entirely inundated, and that cane is still immature. The damage could be devastating!"

"Mayhap, Massa Weldon." Samuel hesitated and glanced at Gilly with worried eyes. "But de fact es," he added, "dere ain't no more cane ta debistate. When dat tide went out, she done took eberyt'ing wid um."

Gilbert's face contorted with rage. Pulling his hat from his head, he threw it onto the ground with such force that Samuel fell back several steps. "It's ruined! My whole blasted cane crop is ruined!" He turned away, took a few paces toward the house, then with his fist raised to his face, stamped back again. "Mark my words," he shouted angrily, "when I find the varmint who broke down my dikes, I'll see to his hanging personally!" Moving with long strides, he walked to the base of an ancient live oak that stood in the front yard and pointed upward. "Right there!" he added. "I'll hang him right there from that branch and leave him for the buzzards to pick clean!"

It took Gilly only minutes to make his way through the woods to the quarters. He found his mother sitting in Maum Beezie's rocking chair staring vacantly at the last glowing embers of the old woman's cooking fire. Her face, though oddly serene, was blanched white.

Laura May and Angel were still awake. Their eyes heavy with fatigue, they sat huddled together upon Maum Beezie's rope-slung bed. Laura May managed a weak smile when Gilly reached down and put his hands to her cheeks, but he could still see the dried tracks of soot-smeared tears on her face. For one so young, he thought to himself, she'd been through a lot lately.

"Mother," he said gently, reaching down to lay his hand on her cold knee, "I'll take you home now." There was a strange and somewhat vacant look in his mother's eyes, as though she had seen something that caused her mind to wander to a distant place. Gilly had seen that look before and wondered if it was some form of self-preservation: a mental escape from the harsh realities of dealing with human beings held in bondage.

Maum Beezie simply shrugged when Gilly asked if she wished to come back to the Big House. It was all too evident that her services were needed here to tend to those who had been injured both in fighting the fire and repairing the dikes. Angel, though still young, pleaded with her grandmother to be allowed to stay in order to help.

"Goodness knows, chil', dis po' 'omans needs all de help she kin get," clucked Maum Beezie as she gently applied some salve to a badly burned arm. "Me oh my, what is dis world comin' to? Us po' niggras gots trouble nough widout tormentin' each udder wid de likes ob dis!"

She turned worried eyes on Gilly. "Gilly, boy, where's yo pappy now?"

"He's down at the cane fields, Maum Beezie. We've got more trouble there, I'm afraid."

"Yes, I know chil'. Well, suh, you gets de 'oman folks home, den you best go he'p dat pappy ob ohnas. Dis be one time he sho' nuff gwanna needs you."

"No, I doubt that he needs me all that much," said Gilly, with a tint of guilt to his voice. "He—well, he and I had a bad time of it in Beaufort, Maum Beezie."

The elderly Negro woman turned and put one chubby arm around Gilly's shoulders. "Chil', you listen to you ol' black mammy. She hain't neber told you wrong, now hab she? Dat pappy ob ohnas, he sho kin be a mighty stubborn man, but he lobe you wid all he haat. Problem is, he jes ain't neber knowed how ta shows et."

Lifting her arm from Gilly's shoulder, she grabbed him by the chin and pulled his face around to hers. "Yemma me talkin', boy? You feel pow'ful angry at dat man right now, but effen you don't go down ta dat cane field, you be jes es bad at showin' lobe as he es! Lobe ain't jes huggin' and smilin' and sayin'. Et be doin'. Et be doin' widout askin' fer nuttin' back. Ohna understand me, boy?"

Gilly nodded, then gathering Laura May in his arms, he escorted his mother back to the house. She followed silently in his wake as they made their way up the dark path through the woods and over the wide lawns to the house. Never once did she ask after her husband or question Gilly about their trip. Nor did she talk about the fire. It was as though she walked in a daze, and this, more than any other event that had happened in the past few hours, filled Gilly with a cold fear of what the future might hold for his family.

Laura May also seemed unnaturally withdrawn. Her face had an ashen look, and her eyes kept darting from side to side as though she expected some unknown fear to overtake them at every step. Gilly wondered if more than just the fire was troubling his sister. When she closed her eyes, did she still see the emaciated, dead face of that drowned slave? Gilly suspected so.

Upon reaching the house, they found that the servants had returned. The candles in the wall sconces and on the candelabra that sat on the foyer sideboard had been lighted. Josephine, her hands swathed in bandages, waited at the top of the stairs with a cup of warm milk ready for her mistress. "Po' 'omans!" she said with gentle sympathy. "She jes hain't strong 'nuff for all dese goin's on." Motioning for Gilly to lay Laura May on the satin settee, Josephine circled her mistress's waist with her strong arm and offered her the milk. Marian simply pushed it aside.

Shaking her head with worry, the Negro cook forced some of the warm liquid past Marian's lips. "Now he'ps you mama up ta she bed, Gilly. Ah es gwanna go back ta de kibbud ta gets a leetul mo' milk fer dat po' chil', but ah be up dere right soon. 'Spect Maum Beezie's gwanna be plenty busy dis night, so's Josephine, she take care ob you mama sheself."

Laura May slumped on the settee and waited for Gilly to return. "Gilly?" she asked as he bent down to lift her up in his strong arms once more. "Will Mama be all right?"

"Of course she will, peanut. Mama's just tuckered out, that's all. Why, as soon as she gets back to Beaufort and her ladies' guild, she'll be as right as rain."

"Gilly, I've always loved living on this island."

"Mm-hmm, I know you have, peanut."

"But *you* don't like it, do you?"

"Oh, I guess I like it well enough."

"You want to leave, Gilly, I know you do." Laura May hesitated, then turned a stricken face toward her brother. "I don't ever want to leave this island. I want to stay here the rest of my life. But—but not like it is now. Not with all this—this badness."

Gilly placed his young sister in her bed and pulled the covers up under her chin. "I know, Laura May. I understand what you're saying. But it won't be like this forever. I promise you it won't."

He waited until her lashes rested softly on her cheeks and the sounds of her breathing told him that she was asleep before he left her room. Tiptoeing silently down the steps, he marveled at the fact that his weariness seemed to have disappeared. He'd find his father now. Perhaps he *could* do something to help repair the dikes. Strangely, he actually hoped that his father would welcome his help.

The work party labored throughout the night, using only the dim lantern light to guide them. Someone had done an all-too-thorough job in destroying the dikes at their most vulnerable points. Timing his work with the high tide, the saboteur had broken down just enough embankment to allow the surge of the sea to complete the destruction.

That it was the work of a small handful of men led by one cunning leader, Gilbert was certain. It had all been done with such precision. And whoever it was had taken a malicious pleasure in destroying, not only the cane, but the land itself.

The forces of nature were forever changing the islands; they hardly needed the help of human hands. Rich soil could be laid down one day and swept away on the next. Sandbars, dune lines, and marshlands could easily be destroyed by a heavy tidal surge or a bad storm. And if a man was an entire fool or extremely cunning, he could misuse those same forces to bring about even greater destruction.

So it had been with Gilbert's few acres of cane. As the flooding tide receded through the broken dikes, it had taken with it good soil and left behind loose sand. Gilbert could patiently wait for the sweeping tides to bring in more silt and muck, but that could take months. If he was to have any hope of recovering the land quickly, he would have to mulch the whole thing over with several thick layers of spartina grass and marsh mud. Such a task would require the back-breaking labor of his entire force of field hands, men and women alike, working night and day for who knew how many weeks!

Sitting slumped in a chair in his study, Gilbert thought about his options. He could forget the whole idea of trying to replant the cane this season, but that thought appalled him. He could choose to leave as scheduled and let his overseer get the fields mulched and then replanted. But that wouldn't answer the problem of ferreting out the one responsible for all of his troubles. That the culprit had set fire to the kitchen house as a diversion was obvious. Should he dare leave now before discovering exactly who it was who was trying so hard to destroy him? Of course not!

The last of his options was the most obvious answer. He must stay on the island for a few weeks more. Not only would he personally supervise the rebuilding of his cane fields, but if it took him all summer, he'd find that devil of a slave who was trying to ruin him. Oh, yes, it was one of the slaves. It had to be. There was no one else on the island but them. For the first time in his life, Gilbert Weldon began to feel that along with the tools of a planter's trade, there was a place for the bullwhip.

A sharp knock on his office door startled him.

"Yes? Who is it?"

The door opened a crack and, the overseer's swarthy face poked through the opening. "Mr. Weldon, I need to talk with you."

"Yes. All right. Come in, Ned."

Ned shuffled his big frame toward a chair but remained standing until the master nodded for him to be seated.

"Mr. Weldon—I—well—I'm pretty sure that I know who it was what's done all this dirty work."

"Speak up, Ned. The faster we rid ourselves of this trouble, the better."

Ned sat on the edge of his chair, his face a mask of anger. "It's that no-count Cudjo, Mr. Weldon. I'd swear on a year's worth of pay that it's him."

Gilbert slumped backward once more and rested his head on his chair. He folded his hands under his chin and sighed deeply. "Proof, Ned. I must have proof." Then he sat up straighter and looked searchingly at his overseer. "You've always held a grudge against that buck, haven't you, Ned?"

"I don't like him any more'n I like a polecat, Mr. Weldon, and that's the truth. He's too smart fer his own good—and shifty too."

"I repeat, Ned, do you have proof?"

"No, not yet—but I'm as certain as I'm sittin' here that—"

"Not good enough, Ned. *I want proof!* Cudjo is the best slave driver I've ever owned. He's worth the price of three prime field hands on the auction block. You want me to hang him just because you've got bad feelings for him?"

"No, sir. No, I don't expect that." Ned hesitated, rubbing at the dirt encrusted in the creases of his hands. Then he looked straight into the master's eyes. "Let me put him in that tin shed fer a few days, sir. Sure as shootin', that'll sweat the truth from him! A few days on bread crumbs and warm water is what that no-count nigger needs."

"Ned, I'm afraid that you're just being vindictive, but the fact is, I want the culprit caught. I want it real bad. If the tin shed loosens their tongues, you can put every nigger I own in it!"

A slow smile crept across the overseer's face. "Ain't necessary to disable every hand on the place, sir. Just give me that Cudjo for a few days, and your troubles are over."

Gilbert watched Ned walk triumphantly from the office and head for the front door. "Hold on, Ned," he called out. "No bullwhip, you hear me? Not just yet!"

Chained by his wrists and ankles to the wall of the tin shed, Cudjo began to discover the true meaning of the word *hatred.* What he had felt before had not been hatred, not in its purest sense. But now with the alchemy of brutal confinement, the base metals of hostility and bitterness were quickly being stripped away. In their place grew a white-hot inferno that the simple act of vengeance could not quench.

Oddly enough, it was the overseer and not the master who was the target of Cudjo's animosity. A man like Cudjo, if not for ill fortune and the West African slave trade, could have become an Ibo chieftain; he understood the dominance of the strong over the weak. Blood and breeding had put the master where he was. Not so with Ned. To Cudjo, Ned was simply an unchecked blemish that had been allowed to grow, a festering mole on the skin of society. The only cure for such an affliction was to incisively cut it away, and Cudjo began to see himself as the surgeon.

The days grew warmer as the sun rose high into a cloudless sky, its bright rays beating relentlessly on the roof of the tin shed until the interior turned into an oven. Weakened by heat and poor rations, Cudjo had all he could do to keep his sanity. But when the sun sank beyond the loblolly pines, and the shed began to cool, he felt his will to resist surge back.

It was when a damp chill began to creep across the dirt floor, and the metal sides of the shack turned from a skin-searing heat to a bone-chilling cold, that Cudjo made his plans. Waiting silently for the quiet footsteps and the whispered voices of those who called him leader, Cudjo knew beyond all doubt that he would win. Yes, it would take some doing, but eventually he *would win*!

Toward the end of each day, when the prisoner's strength was at its lowest ebb, the overseer would arrive and begin his relentless questioning. Only once did Master Weldon come with his overseer. Cudjo quickly detected the uncertainty behind the master's hard eyes. Was it mistrust for his overseer, or did the master simply question his own ability to force out the truth? Either way, this was but another weapon that Cudjo would add to his growing arsenal.

On the sixth day of Cudjo's confinement, a strange event occurred. A messenger arrived from Ladies Island bearing a letter. The master read its contents silently; then, without calling his overseer, he marched to the tin shed and unlocked Cudjo's chains.

Standing sullenly in the overheated shed, the young black man waited for the master to make the first move.

"Cudjo," began Master Weldon, his voice gruff with reluctant embarrassment, "I guess an apology is in order."

Cudjo rubbed at his chafed wrists but said nothing.

"Look here, what else was I to do? I can't have my whole place burned down and torn apart, now, can I?" Master Weldon hesitated, then cleared his throat loudly. "The fact is, I've just gotten a bit of news. Seems that several planters over on Ladies Island have been visited by the same devil—or devils—who hit my place. Sheds burned, mules stolen, fences and dikes torn down—that sort of thing."

Cudjo lifted his head and looked directly into the master's eyes. "And Mr. Ned? What's he say 'bout dat?"

"Ned? Why, nothing—he's said nothing. Actually, I haven't told him yet."

"Hmm. Neberdeless, 'spect he gwanna find some way ta blame Cudjo."

Master Weldon's eyes flickered away from his driver's steady gaze. "No. No, it's obvious that you had nothing to do with it."

"Mr. Ned, he sure got himself a bone ta pick wid me. He know I was at dat fire—doin' mah best to put she out. Ask Willy or Big Jake. Dey seen me."

Master Weldon turned his eyes back to Cudjo's, and once again the black man saw the questioning uncertainty behind them. "Cudjo," he asked, his eyes narrowing, "where do you think Ned was when that kitchen house was burning?"

"Dat be sumpin' strange," answered Cudjo, his face masked with confusion. "Mr. Ned, he wake eberybody up. Send em runnin' to de kitchen house. Den he jes disappear. When he come back, dat kitchen house be gone. He say he done hear some drum-beatin' down in de marshes near dem cane fields. How he hea' drum-beatin' wid all dat noise an' commotion goin' on, I sho' don't know. And how come no one else he'e dat drum?"

A look of concern began to spread across the master's face. "What about the cane fields? How long was it before he got the hands to go down there?"

"Hmm, hard ta say, massa. Some time later I 'spect. Didn' do no good. Too late. Tide'd gone out—took all dem li'l cane plants wid it."

Gilbert Weldon slammed his fist into his hand. He was in a real quandary now. Who was telling the truth, and who was bending it? He began to realize that perhaps only time would tell. Unfortunately, that was a commodity he was quickly running out of. The hot weather was already upon them.

They moved out into the cool shade of a live oak, and Gilbert waited while Cudjo went to the pump handle and drew himself a long drink of water. Then he watched silently as the black man filled the bucket and poured the refreshing liquid over his head and shoulders. Shaking himself like a wet dog, Cudjo returned to his master and waited expectantly. He was not to be disappointed.

"I'll-um, I'll tell you what, Cudjo," Gilbert stammered on the words, "perhaps I can make this up to you a might."

He was thinking fast, trying to find a way to come out even. If Cudjo was telling the truth, he was an ally worth having. But then again, maybe Ned was right. In the flash of a moment, Gilbert decided to play both hands against the middle.

"There's a cabin over there just beyond the stable. Nothing fancy, mind you, but it's a sight more comfortable than that shack of yours in the quarters."

Cudjo's eyes followed the direction in which the master was pointing. A slow smile creased his face. Yes, indeed, this was more like it! Even from this distance he could see that the cabin was a sturdy one: Made of pine wood planks, the building was raised off the ground a good foot by cypress pilings. A small porch with a white pine railing had been attached to the front wall.

"—has wood floors and all that."

Turning back to the master, Cudjo realized that his mind had wandered. "Mm-hmm, sounds mighty nice!"

"I was thinking you might like to fix that place up for yourself. What do you say?"

"Yes, suh, Massa Weldon. Dat'd be jes fine." Cudjo felt the taste of triumph sink from his mouth into his throat. It spread slowly, warming the cold knot in his belly.

"But I expect something in return, Cudjo." The master was getting down to business now. "I'll need those dikes rebuilt and the field heavily mulched before any replanting can be done. I intend to stay on for a few more weeks, but no more than I absolutely have to. The sooner that job is done, the sooner I can get my family off this island. It's the summer months that have me worried. If the culprit who managed all this damage intends to try again, I want to know about it."

Cudjo nodded solemnly.

"Do you get the drift of my meaning, Cudjo? I'm looking for a man who can keep his ears open and his eyes peeled—someone who'd be willing, if necessary, to inform on his own people. If that sort of thing bothers you, you'd best speak up right now."

Cudjo rubbed his chin nonchalantly. "Kyan't think ob de first reason why dat be a problem," he answered with firmness.

"But mind you, if I get the slightest hint that you're stepping out of line, that stint in the tin shed will seem like a campout compared to what I'll do to you!"

It took four weeks to repair the worst of the damage to the cane fields. The work was repeatedly hampered by heavy spring rains that turned even the cotton fields into quagmires. The young cotton plants were first beaten into the ground, then threatened to rot where they lay by the continuous rain and dampness. When the rains slackened up, the air was filled with clouds of stinging mosquitoes. A person could hardly walk out the door unless his body was well covered with thick clothing as a protection from the voracious insects.

It was early morning on the very day of the family's departure for Beaufort that Maum Beezie knocked urgently on the master and mistress's bedroom door. The elderly woman had gotten up several times that night to check on Laura May. The child had seemed so flushed the day before: her cheeks had taken on a red sheen, as though she had spent too much time in the sun.

"Mistress Weldon, best you come ta de chilluns' room," said the old woman, her voice trembling with what distinctly sounded like fear.

"Whatever is the matter, Maum Beezie?" Marian had had a strange premonition that some new trouble still lurked in the shadows of the damp woods, just waiting for a chance to seep its way into the house. She had tried to convince Gilbert to leave the island weeks ago, but he had been adamant about staying until his precious cane field was finished.

The two women hurried to the nursery. Marian stopped in the doorway, her mouth going slack and her heart beating loudly against her chest. She could hear her daughter thrashing about in the bedclothes. Rushing to the child's side, she sank to her knees and cradled Laura May in her arms. The heat emanating from the little girl's moist skin sent waves of fear through the mother. As she turned her face upward, Laura May's eyes flickered once, then glazed over. With a deep tremor she sank into unconsciousness.

Gilbert Weldon, still rubbing sleep from his eyes, entered the room. "Maum Beezie? Marian? What's the matter?"

Turning resentful eyes toward her husband, Marian spit the words from her mouth. "Your cane crop has been saved, Gilbert. Now you'd best pray that your daughter is equally as fortunate!"

"What are you talking about, Marian?" Walking over to Laura May's bed, Gilbert's face blanched as white as the sweat-soaked sheets. "N-o-o!" he cried, his voice breaking into a sob.

"Yes, Gilbert. Malaria! Your daughter has contracted malaria!"

---

1. Lawrence Fay Brewster, *Summer Migrations and Resorts of South Carolina Low-Country Planters* (New York: AMS Press, 1947), p. 5.
2. Theodore Rosengarten, *Tombee, Portrait of a Cotton Planter* (New York: Wm. Morrow, 1986), pp. 50, 51.

4

Somebody's Knockin' at My Door

(1858)

God say, "Sametime dey da pray ta me, A gwine yeh en A gwine ansa um" (Isaiah 65:24).

G illy stepped out into the cool shadows of the chapel's archway. Resting a hand on one of the thin columns that flanked the portico, he glanced up at the clock set into the wall above the outer door frame. Ten minutes past twelve. He waited, as though expecting the doors to open and the congregation to begin filing out. But only the persistent buzz of a mud wasp investigating a crack in the tabby wall below the clock broke the silence.

Turning to lean his back against the column, Gilly scanned the shaded grounds of the chapel. Set within an ancient grove of live oaks, the small Chapel of Ease and its accompanying cemetery had been built to meet the spiritual needs of the planters during their winter stay on the islands. Now, however, with summer well on its way, most of the families had gone inland. Only a handful remained: those with some tasks still needing to be finished, or like the Weldons, those unable to travel due to misfortune or illness.

Hushed and deserted, the little chapel with its shell and mortar walls seemed to sink into the wooded landscape as though it had been erected, not by the hands of man, but by nature itself. Like gray-robed monks on their way to vespers, the moss-draped oaks stood with their heads bowed and their gnarled arms folded as they leaned across the silent graves of the dead. The wrought-iron fence that separated each family plot was draped with low-growing vines and bits of fallen Spanish moss. Knee-high bracken ferns, their lacy fronds spotted with sunlight, grew in the depressions around the grave sites and along the edges of the encroaching wood line. Nature had provided its own verdant benediction.

Seeking to immerse himself in the peaceful beauty of the place, Gilly stepped out onto the shaded walkway. A late spring storm had torn its way across St. Helena Island well after the caretakers had gone. Fallen clumps of the hoary moss and broken branches littered the ground near the chapel's entranceway. Birds rioted in the trees, oblivious to the sacred memory of those interred beneath. A fitting epitaph, thought Gilly, to the well-ordered plans of man.

Making his way between the fenced-off plots, the planter's son stopped occasionally to read the names inscribed on the stones. He allowed his mind to wander as he walked, thinking of those who had gone before. Here they lay, the past generations of Sea Island planters who had dreamed of wealth and power: the Fripps, the Chaplins, the Jenkins, the Capers—each family represented by a line of silent tombstones. "Gone," said Gilly in a whisper. "Their dreams, their plans—gone—like the leaves of last summer—turned to dust."

Gilly felt a hard lump form in the back of his throat. Try as he might to resist them, his thoughts threatened to carry him into the shadowy caverns of guilt and recrimination. Again and again the questions resurfaced. What heritage had these men and women really left behind: their well-tended acres of long-staple cotton, their gracious homes and accumulation of goods, their genteel way of life?

The truth pounded at the walls of his mind, and he had no choice but to let it out. The legacy left by these past generations of planters could be summed up in one word: *slavery*! Rationalized with the perfumed logic of economics and the silky platitudes of social order, it still resurfaced as a fearsome apparition—a rotting carcass devoid of any trace of human dignity.

Yes, and it was this heritage, this burden of guilt, that he must now shoulder!

Shuddering as though the hand of death had touched his cheek, Gilly tried to shake off the morbid thoughts. A sudden crackling noise behind him brought him up short. Turning his head, he looked expectantly toward the chapel's doorway, half-hoping that it would open to a reassuring smile or a warm handshake.

The realization that he was alone with his pain hung heavy on his heart. How desperately he wanted the solace of an understanding friend! Was there no one who could comprehend his plight? Laura May, as young as she was, had often supplied a sympathetic ear. The thought that he might forever lose her devastated him anew.

Again the crackling noise broke the silence of the chapel's graveyard. Tilting his head to look into the tree branches above him, Gilly spotted the source of the disturbance. A twisted oak branch, its coarse, upper bark softened by a coating of green resurrection ferns, hung close to the chapel's archway. From this vantage point, the small, black eyes of a gray squirrel flashed at him. It was a look that, considering the agitated posture of the animal's body, could only be interpreted as anger. Suddenly frightened by the encounter, the squirrel dropped its meal of palmetto berries and scurried higher into the tree.

Feeling sorry that he had disturbed the small creature's dinner, Gilly backed quietly away. "All right, little one. I'll leave you to eat your food in peace." But the incident, as insignificant as it was, only seemed to deepen his depression. Slumping to the ground near an old tombstone, he felt the pain of loneliness cover him like an invisible shroud. Was there no comfort to be found, not even here on the grounds of this familiar chapel?

Turning his head to face the cool stone, his eyes scanned across the worn inscription:

Dearly Beloved Wife of . . .
Died This 3rd Day of October . . .

The words on the moss-covered bottom of the stone caught his attention. Tracing the worn markings with the tip of his index finger, he silently read the inscription:

I am the resurrection, and the life:
He that believeth in me, though he were dead,
Yet shall he live (John 11:25).

Gilly's mind grasped at the words as a man lost in a cavern might reach for a glimmer of sunlight. Pushing himself to an upright position, he stared at the stone with awe. Then with renewed intensity he read the words once more.

How many times had he heard this text, even repeated it word for word while sitting in this very chapel? It had meant nothing to him then, just words marching across the page of his Sunday catechism like so many wooden soldiers.

Touching the worn lettering with the flat of his fingers, Gilly felt a flood of emotion course through his body. A tear, unbidden, slipped from the corner of one eye. Then as though that first was but the check valve of a long-blocked spring, his eyes were filled with tears and his throat was choked with the sound of sobbing. Salty rivulets coursed down his face and dripped off his chin. Unashamed, he let them fall.

Could the words be true? If the dread disease of malaria did take Laura May from them, would a day come when she once again might live? Gilly had never considered himself a particularly religious person. As a child his faith had been just that—childish. He had no reason to question the whys of it. His elders spoke and he listened. Belief was a rote activity: a set of ethics to be memorized like so many mathematical formulas or rules of grammar.

But what had his elders really taught him? More important, now that he was grown, what did he truly believe? Was there a power that could conquer death? The words of a half-heard sermon surfaced from the back corners of his mind. What were they? Something about belief . . . a follower of Jesus, perhaps, or a man asking for healing. "I believe," he had said. Yes, that was it. "I believe, help thou my unbelief."

The force of this discovery pushed Gilly to his feet. He had felt confused and lost when he first entered the chapel's shady grove. Not understanding the nature of his problem, he had felt no hope of finding a solution. But now, in a moment of time the truth had been revealed. His values, his beliefs, all of the say-by-memory standards he had carried from childhood were too shallow to support the weightier burdens that came with maturity. Like a tree without a taproot, he had been stunted in his beliefs.

Now with the imminent death of his sister staring him in the face, he was forced to search for a faith beyond his past experiences. The thought of her death had filled him with hopeless anger. But now that he understood the nature of the problem, the answer was clear. It was here before him—these words etched in stone. With the certain hope of a Saviour, with the promise of a future resurrection, Gilly knew that he could face all of his tomorrows with a calm assurance.

Sinking back down to his knees, he grasped the top of the tombstone, bowed his head, and began to pray as he had never prayed before. He asked the Lord's forgiveness for his lack of faith and pleaded for the power that would bring him renewal. He prayed for his family, desperately asking that whatever the outcome they would be brought closer together. He prayed for courage and for a way to solve the rift between his father and him. He prayed for his mother, asking God to lessen the dark wanderings of her mind. But most of all, he prayed for his sister.

"Please, Lord, heal her. She's so young—so innocent. Don't let her die. I need her—we all need her!"

At last, falling face down on the cool earth, he pressed his forehead to the mossy stone as though the words at its base could somehow burn their way into his memory. Tears flowed freely once more—tears held back for too many years. Over and over he prayed. And when he was done, when he was filled with a silent peace and his mind felt washed clean of fear, he got to his feet and walked quietly from the graveyard.

Stepping up to the mare he had tethered to a tree branch near the roadway, he patted her neck, slipped the toe of his boot into the stirrup, and mounted. Turning only once to look back at the wooded landscape with its small, tabby chapel, he jerked at the reins and moved quietly away.

Odd, but the air seemed clearer now, the leaves of the trees glittered with sunshine, and even the sky had turned from hazy gray to a cobalt blue! Nudging the horse with his heels, Gilly urged her into a jaunty canter that sent clouds of dust curling out behind them. It had been a long time since he had felt at peace with the world!

The horse and her rider hadn't gone more than a few hundred yards down the road, when a shrill whistle broke through the gentle summer trills of a bird song. Lifting himself in the saddle, Gilly scanned the tree-lined edge of the road. "Hey, Zach, is that you?" Placing two fingers between pressed lips, he let out a matching whistle.

"Lawd hab me'cy, de dead be raised!" Zach stepped from the trees, an impish grin splitting his face and a battered straw hat slipping precariously over one eye. "Ce'tain ta goodness you soun' like de trump ob Gabriel 'pon de day ob judgment!"

Gilly smiled, wondering at Zach's words. Had his own thoughts over the past hour been matched by those of his servant? But then again, probably not. Zach had no religion as far as Gilly could tell. Perhaps he had just been mouthing the words of his peers. Reaching down to grasp the hand of the young black, Gilly helped him clamber up onto the back of the saddle.

"Where you ben, Gilly? Dis po' nigger scared dat he gwanna be left ta lib in de woods wid de 'possums an' coons."

"Hah, not a chance! No self-respecting 'possum or coon would have you. Whew, you smell like a dead polecat! Where've you been?"

Pulling his tattered shirt sleeve to his nose, Zach took a deep whiff. "Smells natu'l. Humpf, dat's honest sweat you sniffen', boy." Zach picked at his teeth with the end of a straw. "Cawse," he added nonchalantly, "dat be sumpin' de likes ob you hain't likely ta know 'bout. Now ain't dat de truth?"

Gilly twisted around in the saddle and gave Zach a wry look. This lighthearted banter had been so much a part of their relationship that neither of them took offense. Besides, Zach knew better than to use it in the presence of others. Now alone in the woods they felt at ease, for hcre they could fall into a comfortable camaraderie without offending either the ears or sensibilities of a class-conscious society.

"Hey, where's the rifle?" Gilly asked, suddenly realizing that Zach carried nothing more than his warped sense of humor.

"Left she propped agin dat big oak up yonder."

"How can you hunt without a rifle?"

"'Spect I was 'bout as interested in huntin' as you was," answered Zach.

Ostensibly this trip to St. Helena Island had been billed as a hunting expedition. Gilly suspected that his parents understood the real reason for the day's outing, for they had only nodded as he and Zach left the house. Shaken to the very core by the life-threatening nature of their daughter's illness, Gilbert and Marian Weldon were suffering their own pain and remorse. After the first angry outburst toward her husband, Marian had lapsed into sullen silence, her eyes taking on that faraway look that had so startled Gilly after the fire. His father, on the other hand, was filled with a nervous energy that kept him pacing the floor by day and tossing in his bed by night. His face, as though ravaged by advanced age, looked gray and haggard.

Gilly thought of these things now and wondered what would happen to his parents if Laura May did die. Perhaps he would have to give up his plans to enter the naval academy. After all, he did owe a great deal to his mother and father. But the thought of spending the remainder of his life as a cotton planter only threatened to bring back his depression, so he pushed it to the back of his mind. "One problem at a time," he said to himself. "I have all I can do just to worry about Laura May."

The horse, burdened now by two riders instead of one, seemed disinclined to hurry. Instead of hunting, the boys picked up the rifle, slid it into the leather strap on the side of the saddlebag, and moved on down the road. The touch of sunlight filtering through the canopy of pines and oaks was warm and relaxing against their skin. With his head nodding sleepily, Gilly allowed the horse to take the lead. The mare, seeming to sense the direction of home and a cozy stall, ambled along at a slow but steady trot.

"You feelin' some better, Gilly?" Zach asked, after they had ridden a mile or more in silence.

"Um-hm, as a matter of fact, I am. You?"

"Ya-suh, feelin' fine."

Gilly felt the urge to share his newfound hope with Zach. "I—ah—I stumbled on something back there by the Chapel of Ease, Zach."

"Dat so? Skin you knee?"

"No, Zach. I didn't mean it that way. I meant that I found something—some words that I believe will help me to face what might happen to Laura May."

Zach didn't answer, but Gilly could feel the pressure of his friend's hands tighten against his hips.

"It's kind of odd, Zach, but I found these words on a tombstone. They're—well—they're from the Bible."

Zach remained silent, but Gilly knew that he was listening intently.

"They're the words of Christ. Would you like to hear them?"

"Mm-hm, reckon so."

"'I am the resurrection, and the life,' they said. That's Christ talking. Then—and this is the best part, 'he that believeth in me, though he were dead, yet shall he live.'"

"Who Jedus say dem words fer?"

"What do you mean?"

"He say dem jes fer white folks?"

"Why—ah—no. I guess He said them for everybody."

"Hmm, now dat be sumpin' ta ponder, hain't it?"

Gilly fell silent, but as they moved along the roadway that crossed St. Helena Island, Zach's comment played and replayed in his mind. At first he felt perplexed by the words, but then as he mulled them over he began to experience a certain amount of irritation. Now why was that? Why should Zach's comment have annoyed him? Had the young Negro hit upon a sore spot that lay buried somewhere deep in his subconscious mind?

Neither of the boys spoke again for some time. Cicadas buzzed in the trees, their raspy noise ceasing only when a flock of boat-tailed grackles swept overhead in quest of an insect dinner. Finally having reached the low ground on the northeastern end of the island, the horse and its riders approached the muddy expanses of the tidal marshes. In silence they crossed the wooden bridge that spanned the narrow creek separating St. Helena from Ladies Island. A warm breeze swept in from the northwest and picked up the crackling sounds of thousands of tiny fiddler crabs scurrying across the oozing ground of the marsh.

As they rode down Sam's Point Road toward the Coosaw crossing, Gilly tried to wash his mind of the worries that had tied the muscles of his stomach into a tight knot for so many days. He felt ravenously hungry, and then realized that he had had nothing to eat since breakfast. The fact that his appetite had returned was a good sign. Reaching down into the saddlebags, he pulled out some dried corn bread and a piece of beef jerky, which Josephine had wrapped for their lunches. Handing the jerky and a portion of bread back to Zach, Gilly mumbled his apologies. "Sorry, Zach, guess I forgot about giving you some lunch."

"Tain't nothin' ta 'pologize fer. It be a sad day effen a po' black man kyan't scrounge a meal from de woods and creek beds."

Gilly felt the irritation come back. What right had Zach to refer to himself as poor? Didn't he live in the Big House? After all, house servants had their choice of the best food a plantation could offer. Indeed, he ate every bit as well as his white masters. Surely Zach had no reasons to complain. It wasn't like he lived in the quarters with the field hands and had to grow or hunt for much of his food.

Controlling the small spark of anger that had flared in his mind, Gilly munched on the corn bread and then reached down for the flask of lukewarm water that hung from the saddle horn. Taking a long swig to wash down the dry crumbs, he wiped off the lip of the bottle with his shirt sleeve and handed the flask back to Zach.

"Mighty 'bliged, Massa Gilly, suh."

Gilly's back went rigid. He hated for Zach to call him that. But then perhaps the young black had read his thoughts. Gilly sighed, realizing that an angry response would change nothing. As close as their friendship was, there was always that one impenetrable wall: the unspoken resentment of a slave for his master.

With a certain feeling of pride, Gilly silently complimented himself for holding his tongue. At least he was learning to control his temper. A few years ago he would have jumped all over

Zach for a remark like that. Or could it be? A new and rather frightening thought began to surface. Was he simply beginning to accept his role as slave master?

It was nearly dark when they reached the mouth of Lucy Point Creek and whistled for the boatmen to ferry them across to Coosaw. Sitting quietly on the bank as they watched the lift and dip of the boatmen's oars, Gilly turned to Zach and touched his knee. "Are you really that unhappy with us, Zach?"

Zach waited before responding. "No, I ain't unhappy. It's just—well, how I gwanna 'splain it?" He sat up straight and ran a handful of sand through his fingers. "Reckon you aughta know, Gilly, 'cause you feelin' de same. I hain't a boy no mo'—nigh to man."

He raised his hand and pointed out toward the wide expanse of the Coosaw River. "I look at dat big riber an' wonder where she goin'. Sometime I'd jes like ta start walkin' down she bank— follow de path ob de sun. Mayhap walk right past dat big ol' bank ob clouds off der in de west. Yessu, I jes keep figurin' dat someday I sho would like fer ta be mah own man—mah own massa."

Looking into Zach's eyes, Gilly could see reflected there his own longing for freedom. Yes, he understood. Isn't that what any boy on the verge of manhood wanted? Zach's earlier question came back to him now . . . "who He say dem words fer" . . . but this time with a new understanding.

"Just maybe that day is going to come, Zach. Maybe a lot sooner than you think. You know that the northern states are pushing for the abolition of slavery, don't you?"

"I hear some 'bout dat."

Looking down at the ground, Gilly pushed the toe of his boot into the sand until it made a long furrow. "The South is ready to fight for her rights. I—I think that she might even be ready to go to war over the issue."

"Wahs ain't no good, Gilly. Lots ob good folk get deyselbes killed in a wah."

"Mm-hm, but that's just the way it is."

"If dere be wah, Gilly, you gwanna j'in? You gwanna fight so's de Souf kin keep she slabes?"

Gilly stood up and waved to the boatmen as they poled the

flatbed closer to the bank. "Hard to say right now, Zach. Guess I'll just have to wait and see what happens when the time comes."

It was already dark as they approached the Big House. Lanterns burned in the downstairs parlor and in the master's study. Gilly walked through the foyer, slid open the parlor door, and hesitated when he saw his mother slumped in a chair by the fire. Approaching her on tiptoe he noticed that though she was fast asleep, she still clutched her sewing in her hands. From a distance her face had looked smooth and relaxed. But as Gilly approached her chair and knelt to kiss the back of her hand, he could plainly see the fine lines of worry and strain that crossed her forehead like so many small spider webs.

Marian Weldon did not awaken at the touch of her son's lips on the cool skin of her hand. Realizing that she was exhausted from the long hours of watching at Laura May's bedside, Gilly reached for a knitted lap robe and wrapped it gently around his mother's legs. Then he tiptoed from the room and walked to his father's study.

Gilbert Weldon sat on his big office chair, which like most leather furniture of its day was stuffed with horsehair. He had swiveled it around so that it faced away from the pile of papers strewn across the top of his desk. Staring somberly into the glowing embers of a dying fire, he barely nodded when Gilly entered the room.

"Good evening, Father. I'm back from St. Helena Island."

Gilbert nodded again and pointed to a small armchair. "And how was the hunting?" he asked, his voice flat and hollow.

"It was—well, actually, I gave the rifle to Zach."

"Mmm."

Gilbert Weldon was no longer listening.

"Father, I—I stopped by the Chapel of Ease."

Silence.

"Have you ever walked through the cemetery there and looked at the gravestones?"

"Of course. I could hardly miss them now, could I?"

"No, I guess not. But—I mean, have you really looked at them? Have you ever taken the time to read the inscriptions?"

Gilbert pressed his fingers against his eyes as though the

conversation was tiring him. "I suppose I have, Gilly—at one time or another. Why? What is all this leading up to?"

"There's a Scripture text on one of them. It's the words of Christ. 'I am the resurrection, and the life,' it says. Do you know the text I mean?"

"Yes, Gilly."

"Do you believe it?"

"Believe it? What kind of a question is that? It's from the Bible, isn't it?"

"Yes, but do you really believe it? I mean—well—do you really believe that Christ will come back again and raise the dead?"

Gilbert looked intently at his son, shrugged, and then propped his chin up with his folded hands. "Quite honestly, I haven't given much thought to it. Anyway, who knows how many years away it will be? A hundred. A thousand. What's the difference? When you're dead—you're dead."

"But you would *like* to believe it, wouldn't you, Father?"

Gilbert dropped his fist onto his desk with a thud. "Of course, I'd *like* to believe it. Who wouldn't!" Gilbert could not keep the irritation from his voice. He had so many problems weighing him down; why now, of all times, did Gilly have to pester him with irrelevant religious issues?

Shoving himself abruptly away from his desk, Gilbert looked into his son's eyes. "Listen, boy," he asked, his voice brusque with anger, "what's gotten into you? Have you given up the idea of a naval career? What is it this week—a stint at a theological seminary?"

The sarcasm of his father's words cut Gilly to the quick. Why could they never communicate like a normal father and son? "No, Father, I'm not interested in going to a seminary. I—I was just wondering what you thought about the subject." Gilly stood up quickly and headed for the door. He needed to get away before he said something that he'd later be sorry for.

"Gilly—"

"Yes, Father?" Gilly turned around slowly and waited for his father to speak.

"I—I'm sorry, lad. I didn't mean to sound harsh. It's just that—

well—things are a bit unsettled right now. You know what I mean."

"Yes, Father, I know what you mean." He turned around and stepped into the doorway. "I'll just run upstairs and see how Laura May is."

Gilbert turned his attention back to the dying embers in the fireplace. "All right, Gilly. You do that."

Before mounting the stairs, Gilly looked back at the silent form of his father sitting slumped in the chair in his study. How old he looked, old and pathetic, a man lost in a fading life, with no hope for anything beyond. Gilly shook his head sadly. The anger he had felt toward his father was slowly melting into pity.

The door to his sister's room was closed, but a thin strip of flickering light showed in the crack beneath it. Gilly tapped quietly on the door but received no answer. Turning the knob carefully, he pushed the door open just enough so he could peek in. The stub of a candle stood in the brass candlestand on the bedside table, its small flame threatening to be snuffed out by the breeze filtering through the shuttered windows. The room was full of shadows; only the stark whiteness of the sheets dispelled their gloomy presence.

Laura's small head lay pressed into the goose-down pillow. Seen in the flickering candlelight, her face looked ashen and ghostly. The skin stretched tightly across her sunken cheeks was almost transparent. Her eyes were closed, but even the eye sockets appeared sunken as though death had already claimed its small victim.

Gilly stepped near to the bed and laid a hand on his sister's damp forehead. A pain shot through his chest as he noticed the dark strands of hair plastered to the edges of her face like lanky strings of wet yarn. How lustrous her hair used to be! He thought of her running through the garden, her auburn curls capturing the sunlight, her face wreathed with laughter as she chased the tabby kitten Papa had given her on her sixth birthday.

"Please, Laura, don't die. I need you. You're the only ray of sunshine left in this dismal world."

A low sigh and a movement in the dark shadows on the other side of the bed startled him. How had he missed Maum Beezie?

There she was kneeling on the floor, her head resting on the bedsheets and her big, soft hands wrapped around Laura May's thin right arm. Exhaustion showed in every line of her ebony face, but there was a thin smile on her lips and a bright twinkle in her eye.

"Maum Beezie, your arthritis! You shouldn't be kneeling on the hard floor like that. You'll be crippled up for days."

"No, chil', dis rheumatiz don' matter when dere's prayin' ta be done. De good Lawd, He take care ob deese ol' knees jes like He look out fer dis po' li'l girl chil'."

Gilly looked back at Laura May's face and noticed that the red flush of fever had abated. Pressing his hand to her forehead once more, he felt the coolness of her skin. "The fever—it's—it's gone!"

"Yes, suh, Massa Gilly. An' it ain't de chills what's takin' its place—not dis time."

"Is it over? Has the fever really been broken?"

"Peers so. None too soon needer. Dat was de last ob de quinine I gib her dis ebenin'. I gib her dat dose ob quinine, den I gets ta mah knees and commences fer ta pray. 'Jedus Lawd,' I say, 'de medicine, she's all gone. Now et be up ta You, Lawd. Dis ol' 'omans gwanna stay on she knees till You break dis chil's feber or take she home ta glory. One or de tudder, Lawd. Gwanna stay on mah knees right hey're an' wait fer dat tide ta turn—one way or de tudder, Lawd.'"

"He answered your prayer, Maum Beezie. Do you want to know something? I—I was praying too."

"I figure dat, Gilly boy."

"How? How did you know?"

"When a pusson ben conversin' wid de Lawd, et show on he face."

Gilly reached across the bed and laid his hand on hers. "Maum Beezie, do you know that I love you?" he said with great seriousness.

The smile that flashed across her face was radiant with happiness. "Bless you, chil', I know dat too."

"But I've never said it before," answered Gilly.

"Dere some t'ings what don' need sayin', but 'pon mah word, dey es sho' nice ta hear anysomehow!"

Gilly walked around the bed and helped the old nurse pull herself up into the rocking chair. Then he settled himself onto the floor near her feet.

"Maum Beezie?"

"Yes, Gilly, chil'?"

"Do you believe that Christ will return? Do you believe that He's going to come back to this earth and resurrect the dead?"

Startled by his question, Maum Beezie rocked the chair to the back of its rockers. A look of dismay crossed her face.

"Well, do you?" Gilly persisted.

"Bless mah soul, chil'! You t'ink dis ol' 'omans get down on she rickety knees effen she don't belieb dat?" Letting the chair rock forward, she grasped Gilly's hands. "Course I belieb. Dat's de day ob glory hallelujah—de day ob jubilation!"

"Well, what do you believe about it?"

The wrinkles on the old woman's face softened into gentle lines. Looking toward the ceiling, her eyes grew round and luminous as though she saw something there of great wonder and beauty.

"I belieb dat de Lawd Jedus, He gwanna come ridin' down true de sky on a big gold cloud all made ob angels. His face be shinin' like de sun; His robe all white an' sparklin' wid li'l rainbows like sea foam blowin' off de top ob de waves."

Gilly sat as though transfixed. He felt himself trembling with the excitement of her words. "Go on, Maum Beezie, tell me more."

"Yes, Lawd, glory hallelujah!" Maum Beezie's body was still in the room, but her mind seemed to have been transported elsewhere. "Mah Jedus gwanna come down in dat cloud, an' when He commences fer ta shout, de whole eart's gwanna tremble an shake—gwanna tremble an' shake wid t'under an' lightnin'. Den de grabes begins fer ta open an' de dead come marchin' out. Here come mah dear ol' Jeremiah, only he ain't no mo' wrinkled an' bent wid age. No, suh, his face new like a baby's, his eyes shinin' like mornin' dew."

The old woman reached out her arms. " 'Hey're I be, Jeremiah!' Dat's what I say when he see me. 'Hey're I be!' Jeremiah, he look at me an' smile. Right off I kin tell dat I mus' be lookin' eben better den dey day de Massa gib me to he, 'cause Jeremiah's eyes be glistenin' wid tears ob joy. Den up we go, right true de clouds like two birds soarin' high in de sky."

The old woman fell silent, and the shadows seemed to move in once more. The child in the bed stirred. Her small hand reached up to push back the covers. In a thin, quavering voice she called out, "Maum Beezie—Maum Beezie—are you here?"

"Yes, li'l one, Maum Beezie's hey're. She's right here aside you."

Gilly jumped up from the floor and leaned over the bed. He could see that Laura's eyes were open. A weak smile played at the corners of her mouth. Overcome with joy, Gilly fell to his knees and threw his arms around his sister's frail shoulders. "Oh, Laura May, you're all right! It's over now, and you're going to be fine—just fine!"

"Gilly, is that you?"

"Yes, peanut, I'm here. Both Maum Beezie and I are right here beside you."

Laura smiled at him. "I—I want Maum Beezie to tell us that story again."

"What story, peanut?"

"The story about Jesus coming on the golden cloud of angels."

"Well, bless mah soul, chil', an' glory hallelujah! Course I'll tell you dat story—tell et jes as long as dere be breath in dis ol' body."

It was some time later that Gilly tiptoed from the room. Laura May had drifted off into a restful sleep while Maum Beezie sat rocking in her chair beside the bed, softly singing the songs of her faith with a deep but gentle voice. Stopping at the doorway to listen, Gilly felt the words of a happy spiritual flood through his very soul:

When I git in heben in my elbow chair
    T'ank Gawd I git ob-uh Jerdan
Then I will rock like angel rock
    T'ank Gawd I git ob-uh Jerdan.
        Ob-uh Jerdan
        Ob-uh Jerdan
        T'ank Gawd I git ob-uh Jerdan
One mornin' by de break of day

> T'ank Gawd I git ob-uh Jerdan
> Heard a voice and saw no one
> T'ank Gawd I git ob-uh Jerdan.
> Ob-uh Jerdan
> Ob-uh Jerdan
> T'ank Gawd I git ob-uh Jerdan.
> 'Twas King Jedus passin' by
> T'ank Gawd I git ob-uh
> 'Twas King Jedus passin' by
> T'ank Gawd I git ob-uh.
> Ob-uh Jerdan
> Ob-uh Jerdan
> T'ank Gawd I git ob-uh Jerdan.[*]

Descending the stairs, Gilly decided to go to his father and tell him the good news. There was no need to tell his mother. The sounds of Maum Beezie's singing had awakened her. She stood at the foot of the stairs now, listening intently to the words of the old woman's song. Tears streamed down her face. The vacant look was gone, replaced by the gleam of renewed hope.

Pressing his lips to his mother's cheek, Gilly whispered into the soft tendrils that fell across her ear. "Go on up, Mama. Laura May is waiting for you."

---

[*] Nicholas Ballanta-Taylor, ed., *Saint Helena Island Spirituals* (New York: Schrimer, 1925), p. 74.

5
When I Kin Read Mah Title Clear

(1860)

A gwaine ton de daak eenta light befo dem. . . . A ain't gwine neba lef um alone (Isaiah 42:16).

Gilbert dipped his pen into the pewter inkwell on his desk, positioned the paper at a slight angle, then signed his name to the bottom of the letter with a flourish. "There you are, Marian. It's done. I'll have Jim post it this afternoon in Beaufort."

Marian reached for the letter her husband had just completed. "I'd like to read it first, Gilbert."

"Certainly, my dear. I think you'll find it both informative and to the point." Gilbert pulled off his spectacles. Closing his eyes and pressing his thumb and index finger to the bridge of his nose, he tried to ease the strain that threatened to explode into a full-blown headache.

"Are your eyes hurting again?" Marian asked solicitously as she reached for the letter. "You really should get some new spectacles. The frames on those are terribly bent."

"No, these old specs are just fine." Gilbert set his glasses down on the desk and smiled crookedly at his wife. "It's the curse of old age, I guess."

Scowling with irritation at her husband's heavy-handed script, Marian scanned the page and then set the letter down on the desk. "It all seems so sudden, Gilbert. The child has barely recovered from that last bout of illness. Surely she needs some time to rest!"

"That's precisely why I'm sending for a tutor, Marian. Private lessons will keep her quiet and occupied. Goodness knows, running around through the woods and fields like a wild banshee can't be good for her!"

Marian's eyes flashed with anger. "That is entirely unfair, Gilbert. Laura May does not run around like a wild banshee; she is simply high-spirited. Besides, she and Angel are very helpful to Maum Beezie."

Rising from her chair, Marian pulled a scented lace hanky from her sleeve and pressed it to her nose. "I've been very concerned about Maum Beezie of late. You know, she's not getting any younger. As a matter of fact, she's become rather dependent on the children to find the plants and roots she uses for her concoctions."

"Marian," Gilbert's voice was edged with irritation, "are we discussing our daughter, or are we discussing Maum Beezie? You have such an annoying habit of changing the subject in the middle of a conversation."

"Why, we're discussing both of them, Gilbert. Maum Beezie needs Laura May's assistance to find her medicinal herbs; Laura May needs Maum Beezie's care to make it through these terrible attacks of hers. Don't you see? It's all one and the same thing!"

"We have quinine, Marian. It does an admirable job in reducing the fevers." Gilbert drummed the tips of his fingers on the desk. His head was beginning to throb painfully. "We do not need that old woman's mumbo jumbo."

"Gilbert!" Marian was incensed by her husband's remark. "How can you say such a thing? How many perfectly good field hands has that woman saved for you? Why, through the years her nursing skills and knowledge of herbal medicine have been an invaluable assistance—not to mention her abilities as a midwife."

"Field hands are one thing," answered Gilbert with a steady voice. "My daughter is quite another."

"Saving field hands puts money in your pocket, and money enables you to buy quinine."

Gilbert dropped his fist onto the desk. "Honestly, Marian, I do have other concerns in life besides making money!"

"Well, it was not my decision to stay on Coosaw past the start of the sick season. That was entirely your—"

"Not that again! Will you never let it die?"

Twisting her hanky into a tight cord, Marian pressed a tip of it into the corner of her eye. "I just want you to be a little more understanding with the child. Cooping her up in a stuffy class-room all day will hardly make her more resistant to these repeated attacks."

"I'm not handing down a prison sentence, Marian. The child needs educating. She associates with no one but the colored help. Why, she's as bright as a new penny, but her mind is being wasted on nonsense and old wives' tales."

"She has become an avid reader, Gilbert; I see her at it all the time."

"An avid reader, is it? Humph, more of an avid thief, you mean!"

Walking over to the bookcase that lined the north wall of his study, Gilbert pointed to an empty slot in the neat row of leather-bound volumes on the middle shelf. "Look here. There's a volume missing from my Longfellow set." He turned to look accusingly at his wife. "And how do I know what she's done with it? A child's mind needs direction in these matters, Marian. Education has to be more than a willy-nilly gathering of facts. She must be taught the value of good literature. She must be instructed in the proper care of fine books and—"

Marian stamped her foot angrily. "She knows the value of good literature, Gilbert; that's why she's borrowing your books. And I might remind you that it was I who took the time to teach her to read."

Gilbert ignored his wife's rising indignation. "Secreting my books outside whenever she thinks I'm not looking shows a lack of responsibility. Why, just last week I found that new volume of *Pilgrim's Progress* I bought in Charleston stuffed into a back corner of the hayloft. Thank goodness I found it before the rain leaked in and ruined it!"

Clasping his hands behind his back, he walked toward his desk. "Oh, yes," he said with irony in his voice, "you did a good job of teaching her to read." Then spinning around to face his wife, he added for emphasis, "And if this thievery keeps up, I won't have a book left in my library!"

Marian's face turned white with shock. How dare he talk in such a bull-headed fashion! Was he trying to bait her? "Must you place a monetary value on everything?" she shouted in anger. "It's all so incongruous!" She paused for breath, then launched into her final argument. "And in light of your own vision problems, you might consider the possibility that a forced education could ruin Laura May's eyesight as well."

Gilbert sat down heavily in his chair. "This conversation is becoming ridiculous, Marian! Laura May *will* ruin her eyes if she has to do her reading in a darkened hayloft! Come now, be reasonable. The child needs to broaden her education. I'm not forcing this upon her; she wants it!"

Marian turned on her heels and headed for the door. Turning once more to face him, she made a concentrated effort to control her voice. "All right, Gilbert. Have it your way. Send for this New England scholar of yours. But I'm warning you, if the frequency of these attacks increases, I intend to put a stop to this whole idea of a private tutor!"

With an indignant nod, she turned and walked from the room. Gilbert listened for the staccato tap of her feet as she ascended the stairs. Then reaching across his desk, he leafed through the stack of papers until he found the one he wanted. Placing his spectacles onto the bridge of his nose and stretching their wire temples carefully over each ear, he reread the letter from Aldis E. Thorne, master of humanities and classical languages.

My Dear Sir:

Your letter of November 5th has been received and it is with great pleasure that I may now respond with an affirmative answer to your kind offer. I presume ere this you have received the requested letters of recommendation.

The description of the library available within your home leads me to believe that we will have more than enough material available to complete a grammar school level of education for your daughter. In addition, I will bring with

me several texts on moral philosophy and higher math-
ematics. I shall arrive in Charleston on the twenty fourth of
this month and will catch the steamer to Beaufort on the . .
.

Placing the letter face down on his desk, Gilbert leaned back
in the leather chair and surveyed the neat rows of books with
satisfaction. Despite Marian's reservations, he felt a twinge of
pride in knowing that his daughter, though still so young, was
showing signs of true scholarship. He had always considered
himself a bit of an expert in the area of classical literature. The
fact that his son rarely darkened the door of this study nor
showed any interest for the books therein had always rankled
him. Perhaps now . . .

Dropping his head into his hands, Gilbert tried to push the
dissatisfaction he felt toward his son to the back of his mind. But
try as he might, he could find no redeeming qualities with which
to replace what he saw as the lad's shortcomings. Gilly was like
spindrift blown against a reefed sail—no substance, no real
purpose to life.

Now, Laura May was different. To think that such high
intelligence had been wasted on a girl! But then again, perhaps
she would make something of herself. She certainly had the
spunk and willpower to try. But if Marian was right, if the child
was too fragile to be pushed . . .

The sound of laughter coming from the garden brought Gilbert's
thoughts up short. Pushing himself away from the desk, he stood
up and walked to the window. There in the garden he saw her. With
her white, sprigged muslin dress pulled up above her knees and
her feet as bare as the day she'd been born, Laura May looked like
a wood nymph dancing among the flowers. Surely that wasn't a
frog she was chasing!

Giggling and clapping with glee, Angel sat on a garden bench
watching her young mistress's antics as though they were meant
purely for her entertainment. Neither child noticed the master of
the plantation staring at her through his office window. In a
desperate effort to escape his pursuer, the hapless frog made a
mighty leap, only to land directly into Angel's lap. The black child
was so startled that she let out a squeal and fell over backward.

Laura May stopped in her tracks, a look of wide-eyed concern freezing the muscles of her face. But when Angel rolled over with the frog held firmly in her grasp, the white child doubled up with laughter and fell onto the ground next to her friend.

Still standing in the window, Gilbert shook his head in dismay. "I was right. She *is* turning into a banshee," he said to himself, though he couldn't fight back the smile lines that threatened to turn up the corners of his mouth.

Then as he stood watching, a wonderful thought came to him. The picture of Gilly riding his pony Nutmeg when he was no older than Laura May resurfaced in his mind. That was it! The child needed a pony. A docile little marsh tacky would be the very thing. If it was sturdy enough, it could transport both Laura May and Angel wherever they might wish to go. They could roam the island looking for Maum Beezie's plants and not overtax themselves. And it was the perfect way to teach this carefree daughter of his some responsibility.

Deciding to waste no time with further reflections, Gilbert walked to the corner table where he kept his hat and riding crop. He'd go down to the stables this very morning and have Samuel saddle up his horse. When Gilly was a child, he had had Jeremiah, the head groom, go in search of one of the wild marsh tackys that roamed their island home. But Jeremiah had been dead for some years now, and Gilbert would trust no one but himself to find the right animal for his daughter.

Laura May and Angel had just regained control of themselves when Master Weldon walked out the door and down the front steps. Watching him walk with purposeful strides toward the stables, Laura grasped Angel's arm.

"It's Papa. He's leaving the house." She stood up and lifted herself on tiptoe to get a better look. "I think he's going riding, Angel. This is my chance."

"You gwanna put back dat book you snuk out ta de barn?"

"No, I'm not finished with it yet. But I want to get one that I can read to you."

Angel's eyes lighted up with pleasure. "Oh, Laura, get dat one 'bout de swif' fambly. I like dat story best ob all."

Laura turned around, lifted one eyebrow, and planted her

hands firmly upon her hips. "That book is *not* about a 'swif' fambly,' Angel. It is called *Swiss Family Robinson!*"

"Dat's jes what I said—swif' fambly, only I disremember de robins part."

Laura May rolled her eyes toward the sky. "Come on, we have to work fast. If Mama catches me in Papa's office again, she'll skin me alive."

"What color you be effen you ben skin'd alibe?" asked Angel as she hobbled along behind her friend.

"I guess I'd be red and white. Now hurry!"

"I's hurryin' jes as fas' as I kin go. Bes' I wait right here, anysomehow. Effen you mammy kitches me in dat study, I ain't gwanna be any color but dead!"

Turning once to smile at her young friend, Laura May raced up the front steps and into her father's study. She had no need to hesitate in searching for the book she wanted. With a sure step she walked to its precise location on the second shelf from the bottom, pulled it out, and tucked it under her skirt. But just as she was heading for the door, she heard her mother's footsteps coming down the stairs. Running to the open window, she yanked up her skirts, pressed the book under her arm, and climbed out.

The drop from the windowsill to the ground was no more than a few feet. Laura May landed like a cat. She pressed herself against the side of the house, fearful that her mother might have seen her go out the window. But when there was no sound of footsteps from the room she had just vacated, she sprinted across the lawn toward the garden, where Angel sat waiting.

"I've got it! I've got it!"

"You got swif' fambly robins?"

"No, silly. It's time you listened to something a little more broadening. I got Papa's new book about the seven wonders of the world."

Angel limped along behind the white child as they headed for their secret place in the hollow tree stump at the edge of the woods. After hoisting herself over a row of rosemary, which bordered the edge of the herb garden, she tugged on her friend's skirt and asked, "What I want ta be broad fer, Laura May? I got's me 'nuff trouble movin' round when I's skinny."

The pony that Laura May's father brought back that evening, though a bit shaggy around the edges, was truly a thing of beauty. His mane was long and shiny, and his markings were symmetrical. He was white with a black diamond-shaped pattern at the center of his forehead. There were black markings on his sturdy chest as well as two large, black crescents encircling each of his flanks. His eyes were as bright as the sparkle of the sea, his ears stood erect, and his face showed a gentle nobility.

"He's beautiful, Papa! Oh, thank you. I'll love him to death!"

"If you love him to death, child, you'll spoil him," said Gilbert with an indulgent smile. "Even a pony has to know that his master—or in this case, mistress—holds the reins. Go easy on his mouth with the bit and watch for blisters under his saddle. Treat him firmly but kindly, and he'll obey your every command."

"I don't want to use a saddle or bit on him, Papa. I'll ride him bareback and hold onto his mane."

"You'll do nothing of the sort, young lady. I'll not have anyone saying that my daughter is unrefined!" He patted the pony's quivering rump. "Easy there, young fella." Then, turning to Laura May once more, he waggled his finger at her. "And another thing, miss. You'll have nothing to do with breaking him. Samuel will do that. You don't step a foot into the stirrup until I'm positive that he's been gentled."

"Oh, Papa!"

Within a week Laura May was riding the pony around the stable paddock. "He's got to have a name, Angel," she shouted to her friend, who watched with fascination, her forehead pressed against the wooden railing.

Laura May nudged the pony into a slow canter. "Actually, I should give him your name, because that's what he is, an absolute angel."

Angel stepped away from the cloud of dust kicked up by the pony. Cupping her hands around her mouth, she shouted back to her friend, "I ain't neber heard ob no four-footed angels."

"Well, then, he'll be the first," Laura May answered, her voice high with excitement. She pulled the pony to a halt, then still holding the reins between her fingers, clapped her hands happily. "I know. I'll call him Gabriel. Yes, that's perfect!" Lifting the battered straw hat she had been using to tuck up her hair, she flourished it in the air and bowed in the saddle. "Angel, let me introduce you to Gabriel—Gabriel the pony!"

Angel applauded her approval. "Um-hm, dat's got a nice soun' ta et, Laura May." She made an exaggerated, if somewhat awkward, bow. "Howdy-do, Massa Gabriel, de pony," she said as she winked at the shaggy little creature.

Laura May edged the pony nearer to the fence. "Come on, Angel, let me help you up. You simply must have a ride on him."

"Mm-mm, no way I's gwanna climb 'pon top ob dat wild critter's back." She rolled her eyes in real fear. "First he send me flyin', den he stomp on me. Dis hey're Angel's gwanna stay where she kin feel de groun' under she feet."

But before the end of the month even Angel had mustered the courage to climb up behind Laura May as she guided Gabriel along the sandy river trail that ran from the back of the Big House toward the crossing to Ladies Island. Sitting confidently astride the pony's bare back, Laura May watched her father's boat round the curve in the river and disappear.

"Before long, he'll be going to Beaufort to meet my tutor, Angel. Mr. Thorne will be arriving soon." Though Laura May spoke quietly, Angel could hear the nervous excitement in her voice. "He's coming all the way from Boston just to educate me!"

"Dat so. What's a tutor?"

Laura May nudged the pony back out onto the open trail. "A tutor is a teacher who gives private lessons to a student." Then patting herself on the head playfully, she added, "And I'm the student."

"Mmm. Must be nice ta git all edecated lik-a-dat."

Laura May hesitated before answering. "I guess so, but I'm already very good at reading. Mama says that if I wanted to, I could probably educate myself."

"Mm-hm, dat mos' likely de trut'!"

There was a long silence as Angel toyed with the shaggy hairs on Gabriel's back. "Laura May, I ben worryin' ma head ober sumpin'."

"Worrying? Why, Angel, what should you be worrying about?" asked Laura May in surprise.

"Dis-dis readin' you ben do-doin' fer me," Angel stuttered. "Es dis readin'—well—is et agin' de law?"

Laura May blanched. "Why, no, not exactly. Wherever did you get such an idea?"

Angel hesitated and then answered truthfully, "Gullah Jim, he de one what say dat. He say dat white folks hab laws 'bout learnin' slabes ta read an' write."

"Well, I'm not exactly teaching you to read, now, am I?" Laura May answered defensively. "I'm just reading *to* you."

They continued on in silence for some distance. Though this landscape was familiar, the sound of dry palmetto fronds rustling in the wind seemed somehow loud and disconcerting. Laura May felt a prickly sensation under her collar. She knew only too well that the laws in the southern states against the education of slaves were not to be taken lightly. What would Papa say if he knew she was reading to Angel? But then, isn't that what he did himself when he read the Bible to his slaves in the plantation's chapel?

She tried to rationalize her actions, but something else was niggling at her, and she knew that she must face it. Why was she secreting Papa's books out of the house? Why didn't she just come out and ask him if she could read them? As frightening as it was, she had to face the truth. There was obviously more on her mind than simply reading to Angel. An idea had been battering itself against her brain for days now; she could no longer deny it. The idea was both profound and shocking: she was going to teach her friend how to read and write.

There! Laura May sighed with relief. The idea had surfaced, and there was no pressing it down again. She was going to break the law; what's more, she was doing it both knowingly and willingly. Would Papa be furious? Most probably. It didn't matter. She suddenly felt light and free, as though a burden had been lifted.

Spotting a mullein plant with exceptionally fine leaves, Laura pulled Gabriel to a halt and slid off his back. "Here, hold him steady while I get some of those leaves," she said to Angel. "Maum Beezie's been wanting some mullein for her rheumatism."

Returning with a handful of the large, woolly leaves, she

noticed that Angel was looking at her quizzically. It was then that it happened; the thought that had surfaced in her mind popped out onto her lips. "Angel, I'm going to teach you to read and write."

Angel's mouth dropped open, and her eyes grew wide with shock. "But, Laura May, et's agin' de law!"

"I know that, but I'm going to do it anyway."

Angel put her hands to her face. "Sometime you scare we, Laura May. You scare we more den hags n' hoodoo scare we!"

"There's no such things as hags," Laura May answered emphatically, "and voodoo is all in your mind."

"Dat law ain't all in mah mind. Et's as real as dis ho'se ah's sittin' 'pon."

The white child busied herself with stuffing the leaves into the burlap bag she had carried along. "It's a very silly law, Angel, and I've decided to ignore it."

Angel began to wring her hands in anguish. "Since when kin you jes turn you back 'pon a law what you don' like? Sides, who gwanna ketch de debil when you pappy finds de trut'? Fact es, dis ain't you skin we es discussin', et's mine!" She swallowed hard, amazed at her own brazenness.

Laura May reached up and placed her hand on Angel's knee. "I'm your best friend, aren't I? Can't you trust me about this?"

"Yessum, Laura. I trust you. Et's de udder white folks I don' trust."

Laura May brushed a wayward lock of hair from her face. "Oh, I know what they say, Angel. They think that slaves who become educated will want their freedom; they're afraid of a slave uprising. Everyone is so worried and frightened that they can't even think sensibly."

Taking the burlap bag from her friend, Angel stuffed it under her thigh to hold it in place. How she longed to be able to read. But the thought of what the consequences might be if she was found out paralyzed her with fear.

Laura May pulled herself up onto Gabriel's back, dug her heels into the pony's sides, and guided him down the sandy trail along the riverbank. They had gone but a short way when she began to giggle to herself.

"What you cacklin' 'bout up dere?" asked Angel in irritation.

Laura May tried to control herself. "Somehow, Angel, I just can't see you leading out in a revolution."

The vision of a crippled black child leading a pack of angry runaway slaves flashed into Angel's mind. Despite her fears, she began to chuckle. "Mm-humm, now dat be sumpin' ta see. An' effen I know'd how ta read, mayhap I could jes t'row books at you!"

The girls' laughter rippled across the meadow and was swallowed by the gentle swirl of the waves washing against the muddy riverbank. The birds in the trees stopped their chattering long enough to listen, and then sensing no danger, continued to twitter happily.

"Wait a minute," Laura May said as she yanked lightly on the pony's mane to bring him to a halt. "I think I see a bush of pokeberries over there near that scrub line. Didn't Maum Beezie say she wanted some of those roots?"

"Yessum, bes' I kin recollect she gettin' low on dat too."

Swinging her leg over Gabriel's neck, Laura jumped off the pony and ran through the field of low grasses and broom sedge until she came to the pokeberry bush. Unconcerned with the dirt accumulating under her fingernails, she dug at the roots with her hands. "What does she do with these roots, Angel?" she shouted back over her shoulder.

Angel managed to slide off Gabriel's back. She picked her way cautiously around the clumps of grass as she answered. "Dat's sumpin' good fer de rheumatiz jes like de mullein leabes. Only I recollect dat she biles de roots an' berries so's she kin use de juice on peoples what's got demselbes t'roat problems. Takes down de swellin', she say. Den I 'members one time she done trickle some ob dat juice down de ear ob a field hand what was complainin' 'bout shootin' pains."

Rubbing the back of her hand across her face, Laura May looked up at Angel and smiled. A long smear of dirt was left on the side of her nose and down the length of one cheek. "You're very good at remembering all this, aren't you, Angel?"

Angel's face lighted up with pride. "Um-hmm, dat's what Maum Beezie say. She say I got de gift. She say dat someday right soon I'se gwanna jes take ober fer she."

"Yes, I can see that," answered Laura May. "And you would be ever so good at it." Sitting back on her heels, she surveyed the masses of white cumulus clouds building in the azure sky. "But if you knew how to read, why then you could learn ever so much more."

"More 'bout what?" asked Angel in surprise.

"About taking care of sick people. Papa has a wonderful book all full of pictures of people's insides."

"Ugh! What fer I wanna see people's insides?"

"So you know what needs fixing, silly. How can you fix something if you don't know what it looks like or how it works?"

Angel considered this new thought. "Maum Beezie kin fix people widout knowin' what dey looks like inside."

"Yes," answered Laura May, "but she can't *always* fix them. Sometimes, no matter how hard she tries, she can't make a person well."

Angel pulled her crutches from under her arms and lowered herself to the ground. "Dat de trut'," she answered hesitantly, and then replied quietly, "but when Maum Beezie kyan't make somebody well wid she root medicine, den she pray to de Lawd. Dat's what she do when you was so sick dat you like ta die. She pray ta de Lawd 'cause she know dat He know what you look like inside an' how you need fixin'."

This was a logic that Laura May could hardly argue with. "Yes, I know that, Angel. But—well, it seems to me that—I mean I don't think that the Lord would object if you wanted to know what people looked like inside. Doctors know that sort of thing."

"Maum Beezie, she don' hold much truck wid doctors. She say dat dey jes bleeds people an' gib 'em medicines what makes dem sicker'n when dey started."

"But if you used the right medicines—the kind Maum Beezie uses—" Laura May jumped to her feet in excitement. "If you could read, Angel, you could find out *why* the juice of this pokeberry plant stopped the pain in that field hand's ear. You could see what the inside of his ear looked like! You could see where the medicine went and what it did!"

Angel scratched the wooly curls on the top of her head as she thought.

"Don't you see, Angel? You could take all of Maum Beezie's know-how and make it even better with book knowledge!"

Angel shrugged. "Guess dat's so."

Laura May danced around her friend with delight. "Oh, Angel, let's get started right away!"

Angel's face grew hard. "No, Laura. Et kyan't be."

"Why can't it be?" asked her friend incredulously. "Don't you think I'm able to teach you?"

"Ain't got nuttin' ta do wid effen you kin teach, Laura May, no more den it hab ta do wid effen I kin learn." The black child hesitated as a strange look came into her eyes, a look that Laura May had never seen before. "Der es one t'ing what us colored folk learn from de cradle, Laura May: when de white man make a law, de nigger what wants ta keep he skin in one piece better not break dat law. White mans say niggers ain't gwanna read an' write, well, suh, den dat's de end ob dat!"

"Angel, I meant what I said; it's a foolish law! Besides, who's to know? It will be a secret—a secret just between you and me."

Angel struggled to pull herself up onto her crutches and face her friend eye to eye. "Laura May, you bes' listen' ta some sense. Effen you mammy or you pappy find out I kin read, dey sell me off dis place faster den a rabbit kin hop."

"But they won't know. I told you—we'll keep it a secret. Oh, Angel, it would be ever so much fun!"

Angel shuffled one of her twisted feet along the ground. "It ain't dat I don' wants ta read, Laura. Dere be nothin' make me happier den effen I could."

Glancing down at her friend, the black child could barely bring herself to continue speaking. Her face was a mask of pain. "Gullah Jim, he tell me 'bout dis real smart slabe what learn how ta read an' write. He keep et a secret from his massa a long time. Den one day, de massa call him in an' gib he a piece of paper wid some writtin' on she. Massa say, 'Joe, you take dis hey're paper ober ta de next plantation an' gib she ta de massa.'"

Angel hesitated as she wiped a tear from her eye. "Dis Joe, he disremembers dat he ain't suppose ta be able ta read. He look down at dat paper an' say, 'Massa, suh, which one ob dem mules you wants ta borry? You wants ta borry de strong one or de weak one wid de bad hind leg?'"

Laura May began to laugh. "What did Joe's master say to that?" she asked.

"He say, 'Since you know so much 'bout what's in dat note, I reckon I don' need no mule anysomehow. No, suh, I is jes' gwanna harness you up ta de plow instead, Joe.' An' dat's jes what he done. He make dat po' nigger pull dat plow till he like ta die. Den he take him up ta Charles'on an' he put him on de auction block. De wife an' chil' ob dat po' nigger neber see he agin!"

Laura May sobered. "But Papa wouldn't do that, Angel. You're only a child. Besides, he knows that you're my friend." Laura May stood up and put her hands on Angel's shoulders. "Listen to me. Yesterday, Gilly told me about something he wants to do. I can't tell you what it is because it's a secret, and I know how to keep secrets. But I will tell you this: Gilly says that if something is important enough to a person, then that person has to be willing to take risks.

"This business of your learning to read and write is important to me. I can't tell you why. It just is. And I'm so sure of it that I'm willing to take a risk." She hesitated, watching for the reaction in Angel's dark eyes. "And if you really want to learn, Angel, then you have to take a risk too."

Angel bit her lip and nodded. "Yessum, I understands what you's talkin' 'bout." She turned, and pulling herself along on her crutches, moved closer to the riverbank. Laura heard her sigh deeply.

"Angel?"

"Yessum, I hear you talkin', Laura." She turned around to look at her friend. Tears of happiness were streaming down her face. "I do, Laura. Oh, yessum, I do wants ta learn! I ain't scared ob bein' whipped er even bein' sold off nearly so much as I es scared ob neber bein' nothin' more'n a ignorant, cripple slabe! Will you teach we, Laura? Will you really teach we?"

Laura's smile was as radiant as the sunshine. "Um-hmm, sure will. And we'll start right now." She leaned over to pick up a stick and then walked over to a muddy piece of ground. After smoothing the area with her foot, she pulled the stick along the ground until she'd written a word. Then turning to Angel she said, "Now you take this stick and trace the lines I've written."

Angel balanced on one crutch as she moved the stick along the lines. As she completed each letter, Laura May said the name of the letter out loud and asked Angel to repeat the sound: A—N— G—E—L.

"Do you know what that spells?" asked the white child.

Angel's smile stretched the width of her face. "Dat's mah name, ain't et? Dat spells Angel!"

The sounds of their laughter echoed from the dark waters of the river. Gabriel pricked up his ears and moved closer to Laura May. He nuzzled her arm as she wrote her own name in the mud, and she pushed him away with a nonchalant air. For now their secret was safe. For now only the river and a shaggy little pony shared the dangerous secret of two children who innocently played with an issue that would soon bring an entire nation to its knees.

6
The Slate

(1860)

As you da gwine, God gwine open op you way befo you, fos one step, den de nex (Proverbs 4:12).

Gilbert Weldon, much against his better judgment, finally gave in to his son's insistence that he be allowed to attend the new United States Naval Academy in Annapolis, Maryland. The acceptance came late in the summer while the family was still in the Beaufort house. Elated by his good fortune, Gilly boarded a small northbound steamer with little more than a casual wave to his distraught family. He looked handsome and confident standing on the steamer's deck. The warm sun accentuated the blond streaks in his hair and deepened the tan on his face and arms.

The steamer moved away from the Port Royal docks and headed into the wide bay. Laura May sighed as the boat grew steadily smaller. As far back as she could remember, this was what Gilly had always wanted. How she would miss him, but she hoped he'd be happy. A first-year midshipman could not, under any circumstances, bring a personal servant along to wait on his daily needs. Zach, therefore, had been left behind, and he felt devastated. Gilly was his closest friend. What would the family expect of him now? The mistress had threatened on any number of occasions to send Zach out to work in the cotton like a common field hand. The realization of that threat now seemed all too possible.

Fortunately, Zach's way with the horses finally solved the problem. Master Weldon sent him down to the stables to work as a groom. Knowing his wife's aversion to the young black, but not understanding its source, Gilbert decided that getting Zach out of the Big House was an essential step toward a peaceful homelife.

Laura May moped about for days after Gilly's departure. The few spats they had had now seemed insignificant. The house was lonely and quiet without her older brother. She often wandered down to the stables to visit with Zach, for she missed his ready wit and spunky good humor. But to her dismay, the young black man seemed to be changing. There was a new seriousness about him. It was as though something was working inside his head: resentment, anger, a yearning for freedom—she couldn't tell which. Perhaps all three. Laura May was confused by this loss and change. The news that her New England tutor was on his way became her one bright hope.

Aldis Thorne stepped onto the plantation dock and surveyed his new home with satisfaction. He saw a tree-lined avenue leading up to gracefully sloping lawns. Only the bottom half of the house was visible through the trees, but what he could see met with his approval. Without being pretentious, the house had a graceful appearance. It was a rectangular, wooden structure with a wide staircase flanked on either side by a row of slim white columns. A double-decked piazza, supported and pierced through by the columns, circumvented three of its sides. Massive oaks, their gnarled branches dripping garlands of Spanish moss, shaded the southern half of the building.

Aldis's sharp eyes took in the greeting committee of servants and yard hands waiting respectfully at the foot of the stairs. Standing on the top step was the planter's family: a slim woman with erect head and shoulders and a girl child, his pupil most certainly. The pastel dresses of the mother and daughter stood in stark contrast to the muted grays of the servants' clothing. The colors of the dresses reminded Aldis of a painting he had seen depicting the soft brilliance of a tropical sea.

But it was the servants who held Aldis's closest scrutiny. Having so recently come from the North, where the abolitionist movement was in full swing, he expected to see a horde of underfed Negroes dressed in tattered clothing, living in abject misery. Instead, he saw dignified black men dressed in neat attire and plump Negro women wearing clean cotton dresses covered by neat white aprons. He was aware of the fact that these must be the house servants, and therefore dressed accordingly. But somehow his expectations had run contrary to the evidence now before his eyes. This lifted his spirits. Perhaps this excursion into Dixie would not be the disaster his friends and family had predicted.

Sucking in a deep breath of fresh, salt-tinged air, Aldis sighed with relief. He could feel himself relaxing, as though his body rhythms were already adjusting to a slower pace of life. The weather was ideal: warm days with gentle sea breezes and just the hint of cool nights edged with lacy borders of cleansing frost. A man could immerse himself in such an environment, could become complacent and even indolent. And perhaps, just for a while, that might be enjoyable.

Feeling a sense of satisfaction creep over him, Aldis began to smile. His face, normally so dour, took on a new softness. Pleased with what he considered to be his ability to adapt, he was totally unaware of how truly out of place he looked in this soft southern landscape.

Aldis had New England scholar written all over him. His skin was pale from lack of sunshine, and the deep furrows on his face were marked by the long, blue shadows of northern winters. He wore an outdated frock coat made of heavy black wool. The coat's collar had been turned to increase its life span, but its frayed edges were still quite visible under the unruly strands of dark hair, which sprouted with no apparent order from an almost skeletal head. Likewise, the sleeves of the coat showed all too plainly their excessive years of service. The worn elbows had been patched with a nondescript gray fabric, and the coat's frayed cuffs sat at a level several inches above the wearer's wrist line.

Aldis's trousers, like his coat, demonstrated both age and a decidedly sad lack of concern for fashion. In a day when gentlemen still displayed their calf muscles by accentuating them with slim-legged breaches and skin-tight, pointed-toe boots, the tutor was unquestionably out of style. Not that it would have mattered. Aldis had no calf muscles worth displaying; there was not an ounce of brawn on his entire body.

Josephine, the family's cook, stood at the bottom of the steps and stared with dismay at the tall, scrawny frame of the Northerner approaching her domain. "You ain't gwanna let dat lanky buzzard come inta mah kitchen, es you, misses?" she asked her mistress with a whisper that came just short of a gulp. "A face like-a-dat'd sour de cream an' rancid de buttah, fer ceratin!"

Marian patted Josephine's hand in reassurance, but the closer the man came, the more she felt her own composure in danger of slipping. She had never seen a figure quite like this before: thin, round spectacles perched on the bridge of a nose that protruded from the face like the beak of a bird of prey and long arms ending in bony, almost effeminate hands. But for some reason, it was the white stock collar that repulsed her the most. Standing stiffly upright as it did, the collar only served to accentuate the tutor's scrawny neck and his pointed chin bereft of the redeeming qualities of whiskers.

Marian moaned audibly. How could Gilbert do this to his own child? Had he lost his senses? She could barely make out her husband's expression, his figure outlined as it was by the rising sun. She suspected that on this occasion at least, the changing tide had little to do with a return trip from Beaufort in the wee hours of the morning. Gilbert must surely have wanted to conceal this anomaly of humanity in the shadows of darkness! Having been delayed, however, by a contrary current and a prevailing southeasterly wind, the party had instead arrived in the revealing light of morning.

The master and his New England guest walked up through the row of trees. When they were within a few feet of the house, Gilbert stopped and smiled weakly up at his wife. "Marian, I would like to introduce Mr. Aldis Thorne." Then before she could speak, he hastily added the man's scholarly credentials as though, somehow, they might cover the apparition standing before her with gossamer threads of beauty.

Fortunately, Marian's sense of propriety outweighed her revulsion. Coming down the steps with a stiff, but practiced stride, she stretched out her hand to greet the new tutor. "We are pleased to have you *visit* us, Mr. Thorne," she said, her soft southern accent giving some credence to her forced smile.

If the tutor caught the emphasis on the word *visit*, he gave no sign of it. Flashing a wide smile that suddenly transformed his face from a thing of repulsiveness to something akin to passable plainness, Aldis bent down and kissed the back of the proffered hand. Then noting once more the girl child who was partially hidden behind her mother's voluminous skirts, he stood erect and clicked his heels together. "Ah, and this must be our young student," he said with a quick bow and a clipped diction that was like the sudden closing of a book.

"Laura May." Gilbert Weldon reached out for his daughter's arm. "Come over here and meet your new teacher."

Laura May sidled forward, then curtsied respectfully. "I am pleased to meet you, Mr. Thorne, sir," she said. "Welcome to Weldon Oaks."

Reaching into an inner pocket of his frock coat, Aldis pulled out a small package wrapped in brown paper and neatly tied with a string. He handed the package to Laura May. "This is for you, child." His voice was soft. "A little something I purchased in Boston before boarding my ship."

Laura May curtsied again as she took the package. She could feel the three-sided outline of something sharp and hard. Pulling one end of the string, she undid the bow and carefully opened the wrapping paper. A sparkle of cut glass captured the morning sunshine, reflecting it outward with flashes of silvery gold light. Laura May blinked her eyes and let out a gasp of delight.

"Hold it up to the sunlight, child," said the tutor.

Laura May did as she was told, and with that, a rainbow of brilliant colors flashed across her face. Fascinated by the display, she twisted the glass first one way and then the other. The rainbow expanded and took off as though in flight. Its colorful bands danced through the branches of the overhanging trees and turned the graying strands of moss into shades of blue, yellow, and red. With a slight movement of the child's hand the brilliant band of transparent light hung in the air like a jeweled butterfly. It flitted momentarily across the faces of the servants and then alighted on the white sideboards of the house with such a dazzling display of color that the entire company shouted with delight.

Pressing her hands around the glass, Laura May looked up at her tutor in wonder. "What is it?" she asked in awed tones.

"It's a prism," answered Aldis quietly. "It captures a beam of sunlight, bends it to an angle, and thereby separates it into its component colors." He reached for the glass and once more held it up to the light.

"A prism," he added after a slight hesitation, "is much like truth. One looks upon an object with uneducated eyes and says, 'Ah, this is ordinary and of no value.' But then he takes up the prism of truth and captures all that he sees through its revealing depths, and lo, the blinders of ignorance are ripped away: the rays of his vision are given a new direction. He sees rare and intricate beauty where he once saw only worthless simplicity and loathsome ugliness."

Scanning the assembled company of Negro slaves with the penetrating eyes of a truth seeker, Aldis's attention suddenly caught upon the elderly black nurse who stood slightly apart from the others. A spark of recognition seemed to jump between them, as though each saw in the other a common bond of understanding. Dropping his gaze to the child who clung to the elderly woman's skirts, he smiled gently. The sight of wooden crutches and painfully twisted feet passed over him as quickly as the shadow of a bird in flight.

Aldis turned once more to Laura May. Handing her the prism, he placed his bony hand on her head and said quietly, "Yes, child, truth is a powerful force, for it is capable of transforming the most ingrained of human concepts. But deal with it carefully, for like this prism, if shattered, it is capable of cutting soft flesh like a lethal weapon."

Laura May looked perplexed. She ran her finger carefully along one sharp edge of the prism. What was this strange, wonderful man trying to tell her? Was he seeing the future within the silvery innards of this chunk of cut glass? A premonition of impending danger seemed to press in around her. Shaking it off with a quick nod of her head, she curtsied once more and then stepped back to show her mother the tutor's gift.

Marian Weldon looked down at the prism, then turned to face Aldis. "We shouldn't keep you standing in the hot sun, Mr. Thorne. You must be tired from your long journey. Martin, our family butler, will show you to your room. When you are refreshed, please join us on the piazza. Josephine has prepared some cold lemonade and a perfectly marvelous butter cake."

"Ye-yes, of course," stuttered Gilbert, not sure how to take this gangly northern scholar he had gone through such trouble to import. "I've had one of the bedrooms converted to a classroom. I think you will find it more than adequate. But your inspection of it can wait until you're a bit more settled in."

"Papa." Laura May touched her father's hand shyly. "I'd like to be the one to show Mr. Thorne the classroom. Will that be all right?"

"Why, yes, of course, Laura May. It's as much yours as it is his." Gilbert looked deeply into his daughter's eyes. He could see that she was entirely captivated by this gangly scholar. Pulling off his hat, he wiped the sleeve of his shirt across his sweating brow. "Well, bless my soul, child," he said with delight. "I do believe that I'm finally doing the right thing by you!"

So it was that the dour-looking New Englander became Laura May's mentor and friend. And with his arrival, Laura May's sunny disposition returned. She immersed herself in her schoolwork, for she was an intelligent child with a burning desire to discover all she could of the world around her.

The roomy, second-floor bedroom that had been turned into a classroom became a bright spot in the plantation household. A beautiful globe brought all the way from England graced one corner of the room. A large blackboard had been hung on one of the inner walls, while a well-stocked bookcase lined the other. Laura May had a small desk and a low table, where she did her work.

Aldis Thorne sat at an old, but functional desk made of seasoned oak. His gangly legs protruded at varying angles from beneath the desk. Laura May often giggled behind her hand when she saw her teacher's frayed pant legs and scuffed shoes.

It looked for all the world like the scarred piece of furniture was sprouting matching appendages.

Indeed, Aldis had his own sense of humor stimulated on more than one occasion, for he was not unaware of the periodic gaps in the well-stocked bookcase. Like missing teeth, they told the tale of stolen sweets used to fill the cravings of a voracious appetite. And then there was that small black face that so often appeared in the crack of the classroom doorway. At times, even when his back was turned, he sensed quizzical eyes watching him from the darkened hall.

All of this had its own peculiar effect on the tutor. Aldis gradually adopted a sort of tunnel vision that obliterated any small but acceptable distractions. And though it put a strain on his vocal cords, he found himself raising his voice several decibels so that he could be heard even through shut doors.

A heat wave in mid-autumn brought with it an increase in humidity. The upstairs classroom became too stuffy for clear thinking. It was Laura May who came up with the suggestion that they temporarily move their operations onto the piazza. But even there the warm sunshine sent rivulets of sweat trickling down their spines.

"Mister Thorne," said Laura May one day when the temperature had climbed into the high eighties and not a breath of air stirred. "Why don't we go down to the lower piazza? The front deck is shaded by the oak trees, and it would be ever so much cooler down there."

Aldis thought it a good idea. Master Weldon agreed and had the house servants move a table and two chairs to the lower front piazza. Thus it was that Laura May conceived the idea that would bring the direct benefits of a trained teacher to the hungry mind of a crippled slave girl.

It was all done, of course, in the greatest of secrecy. Well before each daily lesson began, Angel would slip quietly under the cassena bushes that bordered the lower piazza. Armed with a small slate and a piece of chalk, she tried to follow the writing and arithmetic lessons with her own squiggly lines. Laura May waited until Mister Thorne's nose was pressed into a book; then she would slip a paper or two through the piazza railings. It all proved quite easy, for, to the tutor's credit, he had a way of lowering his head at the most opportune times. If his eyes were sparkling with amusement when he reemerged, his student could only assume that he found some bit of pleasure in his reading material.

Weekends and late afternoons were times of leisure for both tutor and student. And as much as Aldis enjoyed teaching this bright child who had become his pupil, those hours when he could stretch out on his cot and catch a few extra winks of sleep or bury himself in a new book or a scholarly journal were much prized. He wasn't much for exercise, though the wooded trails and tidal beaches offered a host of opportunities. Aldis found both his pleasure and his relaxation in a continuation of personal study.

This was not the case for Laura May. How she loved those times when she could run free in the open sunlight! Astride Gabriel, with Angel perched behind her, Laura May ventured farther and farther from the Big House in search of Maum Beezie's medicinal herbs and roots. And on many such a day she concealed under her skirt the books that would further Angel's growing storehouse of knowledge.

A muddy riverbank was their favorite outdoor classroom. Angel could practice writing the new words and sentences she was learning in the firm mud, and when the tide came in, all evidences of her lawbreaking activities were neatly washed away. Sitting under the sheltering branches of a thick palmetto, she would read aloud to her youthful teacher, patiently accepting both the instruction and criticism that were so eagerly given.

Unfortunately, complacency has a way of setting in when all is going smoothly, and with complacency comes carelessness. It was a warm morning in late October when disaster struck. Angel had scuttled under the cassena bushes a bit late that day, for the house servants were packing the family's belongings in preparation for the move back to Beaufort; she had had difficulty in getting away.

Pushing her crutches to one side, she settled herself onto the bed of dried leaves and pine needles that she had piled together to avoid sitting in the dirt. She pulled her slate from under her skirt and took out the bit of chalk that she had tucked into her waistband earlier that morning. The piazza was still deserted, so she decided to practice her writing while she waited. Pressing the chalk onto the slate in a determined manner, she began to write:

I is happy becawz I can read and write.

No, one of the words looked wrong. "Bee-caaw—zz." Angel said the word to herself several times, dragging out its sound in an effort to find the solution to its spelling. "Well, it sho'nuff sounds right," she said to herself. But it still did not look right. She kicked at one of her crutches in frustration, and it slid across the slippery pine needles until its tip projected out from under the bushes. She ignored it. There was plenty of time to pull it back.

Wiping the offending word out with the flat of her index finger, she bit down on her tongue and scratched the chalk into the slate as hard as she could. *"Be-caw-se."* There, that looked better. Then still applying enough pressure to scratch the slate, she wrote her name in capital letters. *ANGEL*. She felt a measure of pride as she looked over the words she had just written. Yes, she was learning fast now.

Heavy footsteps coming around the side of the house caught her attention. Angel sucked in her breath and held it. The footsteps came nearer, then stopped. There was a long, breathless silence.

"Now what hab we hey're?"

It was Cudjo!

The crutch that she had so carelessly kicked away was suddenly lifted out of sight. Angel pressed herself against the wooden slats at the base of the piazza, but it was too late. A strong black hand reached under the bushes, grappled through the dried leaves, and grasped at her ankle. Angel tried to pull her foot away, but the hand bit into her flesh like a metal vise.

"Le'me go! Le'me go!" she yelled, her voice trembling with fright.

Cudjo's laugh was low and dangerous. "Now ain't dis a stroke ob luck," he said as he dragged the child from under the bushes. "An' jus' when I was hongry 'nough ta eat me a 'possum. Now I kin cook me up some tender, young coon meat instead!"

Angel gaped at Cudjo's smirking face and felt certain that he meant just what he said. He did look mean enough to eat children! But Cudjo was staring at something else; he was looking down at the slate that she still clutched tightly in her hand. Angel tried to stuff the slate under her skirt, but it was too late.

"Give me that, you no count, crippled niggra!" Cudjo yanked her up by the wrist and forced open her hand. The slate dropped at his feet. Angel began to cry, but not even the tears of a child reached this man who had long since hardened his heart to all thoughts of human compassion.

Cudjo could not read, but he knew instantaneously what he was looking at. A leering smile slithered across his face like a poisonous serpent. It had been a discouraging week. The overseer had severely reprimanded him for the slack work done in weeding the lower cotton fields. Worse yet, Ned had long suspected him of the destruction of the cane fields and was still nosing around for evidence. If he ever managed to shake the truth from the right field hands, he would destroy Cudjo's hard-won standing with the master.

Now here was this chit of a girl handing him a little piece of information that could turn circumstances to his advantage. For whatever Cudjo lacked in learning, he more than made up for with cunning. The convoluted workings of his mind were going at full tilt. His past experiences with voodoo had been disastrous, but he was still a firm believer in the arts of black magic. His mistake had been using the wrong practitioner. That conjure doctor over on St. Helena had played him for a fool.

Cudjo still felt the same cold shudder run through him when he thought of Phoebe's untimely death. Despite Samuel's obvious love for the stunningly beautiful mulatto, Cudjo had managed to extract a promise from the master that it was *he* and not Samuel who would be her chosen mate. The fact that Phoebe loved Samuel and not him hadn't mattered in the least. He wanted her!

But just to be certain, he had gone to visit the old conjure doctor on St. Helena. Cudjo hoped the wily old necromancer could put a death curse on his rival; then Phoebe's lovesick foolishness would be quickly brought around to a new tack.

How had things gone so wrong? Had Dr. Buzzard misunderstood him, or had that son of the devil simply found pleasure in making sport of him? There was no question that the witch doctor's black magic was powerful. Unfortunately, it had killed the wrong person. When Cudjo returned to the plantation early the next morning, he had found the people of the quarters mourning, not Samuel's death, but Phoebe's!

Yes, he had been made to look like a fool. Dr. Buzzard had, in effect, hung him with a rope of his own making. Then he'd left him twisting in the wind to be pecked at by those black birds who lived in the slave quarters. The defeat was humiliating, and he wanted revenge. Now he'd have it: revenge, and a lot more! Who could imagine that a small, crippled child could be such a useful weapon!

Better yet, Cudjo found a certain humorous irony in the fact that it would be none other than Maum Beezie who would supply the missing ingredients to his deadly plot. As a dedicated root worker and a respected elder of the slave community, she would never be suspected of being an accomplice to murder. Nor did Cudjo have any doubts about his ability to suck the old woman into the center of his hellish sinkhole. She was, after all, Angel's grandmother and guardian; she would do everything in her power to see that no harm came to the child.

Cudjo let go of his vicelike grip on Angel, but he kept both the slate and the small crutch tucked tightly under his arm. "Get yo'self back ta de quarters where you b'long, cripple girl. I ketch you snoopin' 'round hey're agin an' you gwanna find more twisted den jest you feet!"

Angel didn't wait to find out what more he might do to her. She hobbled away on one crutch as quickly as she could. Cudjo watched her labored progress with satisfaction. He liked the feeling of power it gave him to see these worthless niggers cringe in his presence. If only the master realized the full potential of his leadership abilities. Ned couldn't begin to get the kind of work out of these ignorant slaves that he could.

Cudjo rubbed at his chin and examined the marks on the slate. Perhaps he could spike two cooters on one stick and roast both of them at the same time. He hated the overseer and was determined to be rid of him, but what about Maum Beezie? She had been a fly in his molasses jar for too long. Yes, this was his chance to get even with the lot of them.

Resting the crutch on one shoulder, Cudjo started off for his cabin with a ground-eating stride. He thought about the old woman as he walked. The few times he had contemplated going to her for help in the past had come to nothing. She had brought him to understand in no uncertain terms that she would have no truck with black magic or voodoo. What a fool she was, spouting her worthless godliness as though she was on the verge of sainthood! Well, let's see how godly she is when she knows her granddaughter's life is in jeopardy, he thought to himself with smug satisfaction. Yes, it would be she who would be spinning in the wind then!

It was already dark when Cudjo approached the tabby cabin at the edge of the slave quarters. He carried the small crutch, but he had effectively secreted away the incriminating slate. He wondered if the crippled girl had gotten up enough nerve to tell her grandmother exactly how she had lost her things.

Then just as Cudjo reached the doorway, a new thought came to him. Would Maum Beezie know about the slate? Most likely not. The child surely must realize that she was breaking the white man's law in trying to learn how to read and write. Would her grandmother go along with such an action? Of course not! She had too many uppity scruples for that sort of thing.

He hesitated before knocking. He had to think this out. Should he change his planned approach? No! This new realization made things all the better. If he could first shock the old woman, it would be just that much easier to squeeze what he wanted from her. Raising his fist to the door, he pounded with such force that even the oak door frame shook.

Angel had already crept into her small bed when the knock came. Maum Beezie, sitting comfortably in her chair by the fire, jumped with a start at this loud intrusion on her private thoughts. Sure that this must be some dire emergency, she called out for the visitor to enter.

Whether Cudjo heard her or not hardly mattered. He yanked

open the door and in three long strides reached the hearth. Maum Beezie rose from her chair in fright. Her first reaction was to place herself between this evil man and her granddaughter, though she had no idea that it was indeed the child whom he threatened.

Cudjo pulled one of the master's cigars from his shirt pocket, leaned over and plucked a straw from the old woman's broom, then shoved the end of the straw into the flames until it smoldered and caught fire. With a nonchalant air he lighted the cigar, took several long puffs, then purposefully sat down in Maum Beezie's rocking chair and propped his booted feet on top of an andiron.

Too stunned to remonstrate at Cudjo's forward behavior, Maum Beezie leaned heavily against the wall and waited for him to speak. From the corner of her eye she could see Angel cowering on the far side of the bed. Having noticed earlier that the child had come home with only one crutch, she had asked for some enlightening explanation. But Angel's vague statement about accidently losing the crutch somewhere in her wanderings could hardly have given the elderly woman the first clue that even greater trouble was brewing.

Cudjo blew out a few puffs of foul-smelling smoke and examined the glowing tip of his cigar. He was enjoying this. "Ol' 'omans," he said, putting emphasis on the Gullah speech patterns, "'spect you es wonderin' why dis slabe driber heself come knockin' on you door."

Maum Beezie didn't respond. It never ceased to amaze her how easily this man could change his way of talking. When he spoke to someone like the overseer, his English was every bit as good as the master's. When he spoke to the master, his Gullah was a slow and respectful shuffle. But when he talked to the Gullah people themselves, ah, that was a different matter. Then he would twist the musical dialect into something derisive and shameful, like one might talk to a dog, using short words and half-sentences.

"You see dis ceegar, ol' 'omans?" Cudjo took a long puff on the cigar and blew the smoke out through pursed lips. "De massa heself done gib me dis ceegar. You know why massa done dat?"

Maum Beezie gave him a cold stare but refused to be drawn into his trap.

Unfazed by her lack of responsiveness, Cudjo went on. "He gib me dis 'cause he trus' me. He know dat Cudjo ain't gwanna bring he no grief. No, suh, Cudjo, he hab a heap ob respec' fer de massa's prope'ty an' sho ain't gwanna bring he no grief."

This was more than the old woman could take. "Dat's enough ob you onrablin' you mouf, Cudjo. Effen you come hey're ta ramble 'round de briar patch, Cudjo, you sho done chose de wrong time. Whatsomeber be eatin' at you innards, you best spit she out right soon afor I call fer de obasheer."

"Uh, uh, 'ol 'omans, you ain't gwanna do dat. De obasheer be de las' pusson you es gwanna want in dis hey're cabin. Mr. Ned don' like folks what ain't gwanna gib de massa respec'. An' he sho' don' likes no uppity niggras what t'inks dey kin break de buckra's laws."

"What you goin' on 'bout, Cudjo? What laws you talkin' 'bout?" Maum Beezie could hear Angel's stifled sobs.

Cudjo dropped his booted feet to the floor with a thud and sat up straight. He flicked the ashes from his cigar into the fire and riveted the old woman in place with a hard glare. "De law what say no niggra slabe kin learn readin' an' writin'. De law what say dat uppity niggras what learns ta read an' write aughta be hung by dey neck till dey daid—er skinned alibe—er sold off. You know 'bout dat law?"

Maum Beezie could feel a cold sweat forming on her brow. "Course I know 'bout dat law."

"Den you bes' tell dis li'l cripple niggra settin' ahind you 'bout et, 'cause she ain't seem ta he'r tell ob dat law."

With this Angel began to sob in earnest. "I didn' mean ta break no law, Maum Beezie," she wailed. "Laura May, she say dat et was a bad law. She say peoples shouldn' hab ta obey laws what ain't no good."

Cudjo was taken aback by this last bit of information. He had never considered the possibility that the master's own daughter was involved in this little scheme. It put a whole new light on things, and he'd have to tread mighty carefully, or he'd find himself on the wrong end of the stick. Covering his thoughts with derisive laughter, he stood up and walked to the bed where the black child cowered.

"You think the master's gwanna listen to talk like dat 'bout his own child?" Cudjo dropped all pretense at speaking Gullah and spit the words into Angel's face with such force that she fell over backward. "Listen here, you little toad; I'll tell you exactly what the master's gwanna do. When I tell him that you've been hunkerin' down in the bushes by the piazza so's you can learn readin' an' writin', he's gwanna sell you off this place faster than you can blink your eyes. Why, he'll pack you up an' send you so far away that not even the devil himself will know where you is!"

Then he spun around on the balls of his feet and faced Maum Beezie. Jamming the cigar back into his mouth, he dropped his voice and talked through clenched teeth. "And as for you, old woman, you'll never see this brat again, not as long as you live." Spitting a fleck of tobacco leaf onto the floor, he ground it down with his heavy boot and then added, "Of course, you probably won't live much longer anyhow—not after they've taken this crippled cur away from you."

Maum Beezie, her eyes wide with fear and revulsion, backed away from the onslaught of Cudjo's words. Was it true? Had Angel really done that?

The memory of a long-suppressed horror came back to her. She saw in her mind's eye a young black man, whom as a girl she had greatly admired. He was tall and as slender as a reed, carrying himself with such nobility that even the white folks nodded and smiled when he talked. But it was his eyes she remembered the most, for they had fairly sparkled with intelligence and a hunger for learning.

Michael, that was his name. A good name. A good man. How he had learned to read she never knew, but he had. And she was still just a girl when the dreadful thing happened. He had come to the quarters to read to the people from the Bible. Yes, she could even remember the words of his text. Oh, not just the way he had read them; the crisp English words were long forgotten, and in their place had come the easier sounds of Gullah. How many times since then had she said the words over to herself? But now—now she needed them more than ever:

De Lawd, He me shepud!

Her mind pulled at the words, and she wrapped them about her like a protective coat of armor:

I hab eberyting wa I need.
He mek me fa res een green fiel
En He lead me ta still wata
wa fresh en good fa drink.
He tek me soul en pit em back weh he spos ta be.
He da lead me long de right paat,
For He name sake, same lika He binna promise.

Those beautiful, intelligent eyes! The horror of what happened to them still sent shivers of soul-searing pain through her. They had put them out with a hot poker—had strapped him down and burned out his beautiful eyes!

Aaldo I walk tru de wally a de shada a deat
I ent gwanna faid no ebil, Lawd,
Cause You dey longside me.
You rod an You staff protec me.

That's what he'd said as they dragged him to the base of an oak tree. They'd put a noose over his head and yanked it up until all could see his ruined face. "This is what happens to niggers who learn to read!" they'd said. But still his words went on:

You don papeah nof bittles fer me,
Weh all me ennyme kin shum.
You gib me haaty welcom.
You nint me hed wid ail
En fill up me cup tel he run oba.
Fa true, You gwanna lob me
En tek cyah a me long es I lib.

Cudjo was leaning into her face again, saying something about poison. What was it he wanted? Poison to kill a skunk?

Was that what he wanted?

"You do that for me, old woman, and the slate disappears like it never happened. You do that, and we're even. You'll keep your granddaughter. You'll never have to—"

Oh, poor Michael and his ruined face, his mouth still trying to form the words as the last breath of life was choked from him!

En I gwanna stay ta You house fareba. Amen!

Maum Beezie turned her tear-stained face toward Angel. She reached out her arms, and her granddaughter hobbled into them.

"Dis true, chil'?" the grandmother asked. "Kin you read lika he say you kin?"

"Not so bery good," answered Angel through sniffled tears. "Jes a li'l, but not so bery good."

"Um-hmm." Maum Beezie leaned over and kissed the top of Angel's head. "Well, chil'," she said quietly, "nex' time weuns goes ta de Big House ah es gwanna borry de massa's Bible. Sumpin' I wants you ta read ta me from dat Bible. Et starts out lika dis: *De Lawd, He me shepud!*"

---

* From the Gullah translation of Psalm 23. Sea Island Translation and Literacy Project, St. Helena Island, South Carolina.

7

The Grave Marker

(1860)

De powa ob de wickedy people ain't gwine las faeba, Bot de Lawd keep on a gibe strengt ta dem wa do wa E want um fa do (Psalm 37:17).

Gullah Jim twisted his fish line around the branch of a tree so that the mess of mullets dangling at its end hung well above the ground. Cocking his head to one side, he listened intently to the sounds of the woods. The rustling of cotton rats scurrying through grassy tunnels, the grumbling croak of a nearby frog, and the noisy chirping of a cricket choir all broke through the darkness.

In the distance, a mockingbird let out a long trill, ending with a burst of song. From up on the ridge came the faint rustling sounds of a herd of deer as they pawed at the leaf-strewn floor of the forest in search of acorns and berries. These woodland noises were familiar and comforting to Jim—they were not the source of his uneasiness.

After hooking his hat on the blunt stub of a broken sapling, the old man made a quick survey of the moonlit landscape. Why, he wondered, was he filled with such apprehension? Had he actually heard something, or was it simply a premonition of danger that filled him with tension?

Jim believed in his premonitions. They were like voices talking in his head. He could recall any number of occasions when he had managed to save his hide by listening to his head. But then

107

again, maybe the master was right. "It's a sixth sense you have, Jim," he had said. "There's nothing magical to it, but I can't think of another man I'd rather have near me when trouble's brewing."

And that's just what his sixth sense was telling him now. Trouble was brewing, real trouble, the kind that brought a cold sweat to one's brow and sent shivers through his stomach. To make matters worse, it was nearby.

Hunkering down so he was sitting on the backs of his heels, Jim pressed his hand to the earth. There was a warmth to the ground, as though a bit of sunlight had been captured beneath the thin layer of topsoil. He brushed at the damp leaves and prickly pine needles to release the earthy scents of decaying vegetation and dried resin. His nostrils flared wide. These were good, clean smells, comforting to his troubled spirit. Jim began to relax.

Pushing himself upright, the old man was just about to retrieve his mess of mullets when his sharp ears caught the unmistakable sound of human laughter. There was nothing humorous in it—just a low, menacing snicker that drained out from under the doorway of the nearby cabin like polluted water from a flooded ditch.

Jim's blood turned to ice. This sound was not right for a night peaceful with hazy moonlight. It had nothing to do with the sleepy twittering of birds and the happy chirping of crickets. And under no circumstances was it appropriate for this particular tabby cabin where a woman the likes of Maum Beezie lived.

Moving with a lithe grace that belied his advanced years, Jim crept toward the cabin. He was about to press his ear against the rough exterior of the door when his stomach set up a traitorous rumbling that caused him to flinch and step backward. Beezie must have boiled up a pot of yard stew for supper, he thought with frustration. One more whiff, and the succulent smell of it would do him in for certain.

As always, Jim had worked up a powerful appetite with his day on the river. And having been successful at fishing, he could afford to spend his return journey in happy ruminations of his pending dinner. His step had been light as he had walked down the woodland trail, for he was thinking happy thoughts of Maum

Beezie's mullets and rice with a little clabber on the side.

But now, abruptly, his dreams had vanished. Feeling like a loose sail caught in a sudden gale, he gave a yank to the rope that held up his trousers and sidled quietly back up to the doorway.

Yes! There it was again, the same cold laughter. Jim tensed his wiry little frame and contemplated his next move. The voice was unmistakable. Cudjo! Now what would that no-count slave driver be up to at this time of night?

Hunkering down once more, he pressed his ear to the crack at the bottom of the door. Then he turned his head so his left eye was close to the crack. A thin stream of light flickered and danced across the hard-packed dirt floor, but he could make out nothing more.

There had been a pause in the conversation, as though the last speaker was waiting for a response. Then suddenly Cudjo's voice reverberated against the oak doorway. The gist of the conversation was all too obvious. Jim felt the hair on his neck bristle with anger.

Cudjo's voice was plain now. He outlined his demands in a clipped, businesslike tone, then waited for a response. Jim felt certain that both Maum Beezie and Angel were present, but neither one of them seemed inclined to answer her tormentor. Relentlessly Cudjo's hard voice went on, describing the full extent of Angel's "crimes" and detailing with vivid clarity a gruesome list of probable punishments.

Jim stayed at the doorway until the movement of Cudjo's booted feet cut off the thin stream of light. Then still on his hands and knees, he worked himself around the corner of the cabin and hid amongst the dark shadows on its north side.

"Dat mis'able varmint!" he muttered under his breath. "Bad 'nuff he'uns gots ta ruin an ol' man's bitals, now dere he be b'ilin' up his own mess ob fish an' deblin dat po' ol' 'omans." He scraped his hand across his bristly chin in frustrated anger.

Jim could feel rage working up through his stomach, squeezing the hunger right out of it. The fact that the driver was trying to inflict a despicable form of blackmail on Maum Beezie was one thing. The far-reaching extent of it, however, was more than Jim could fathom. Black men had turned against their own people before; there was nothing unusual to that. But how could a man abuse a motherless, crippled child in such a manner? Had he no compassion, no sense of decency? Jim had half a mind to break down the door and throw the traitor out on his ear. But instinct told him that he must be both patient and cautious.

With his mind racing, the old fisherman tried to come up with a plan. What if he was to shadow Cudjo for a while? How difficult would it be to discover where the driver had squirreled away his evidence?

Jim scratched his ear in contemplation, then despite his anger and apprehension, began to smile. The fact that there was a certain sport in outwitting this rat before he could chew a hole in the woodwork put a different light on things. It was like hooking onto some monstrous fish, who, if you didn't know what you were about, could pull you overboard and drown you. "Play out de line, Jim," he said to himself. "Jes play out de line. Let she hit de bottow." Given enough time, the old man knew that his quarry was sure to resurface.

Cudjo's heavy footsteps approached the doorway. Jim pressed himself hard against the rough outer wall of the cabin. Broken bits of oyster shell stabbed at his spine, but he ignored them. Closing his eyes so not even their whites could reflect the moonlight, he silently waited for Cudjo to open the door.

He did not have to wait long. Cudjo grasped at the latch, then when it failed to yield to the pressure of his hand, slammed it hard with the side of his fist. Simultaneously he gave the door a mighty kick. It flew out on its leather hinges accompanied by the sounds of splintering wood.

Unfazed by the damage he had wreaked, Cudjo tapped the end of Angel's crutch on the broken doorframe. He took a deep breath of the night air and exhaled, as though exhilarated by its freshness. "Right purty evenin', now ain't it!" he exclaimed, putting sarcastic emphasis on the Gullah speech patterns.

The driver examined the small crutch as though looking for flaws. "Yessum, you-all'l find dat ah am a compass'nate man—so long's ah ain't crossed none. Now take dis li'l ol' crutch, fer 'zample. Got anudder'n jes' like she tucked 'way fer safe keepin'. No point in holdin' on ta bof of em, now, is dere?"

He turned as though expecting an answer. When none came, he leaned over and slid the crutch across the dirt floor of the cabin. It landed with a thud against something solid, but no one moved to retrieve it.

Snorting with anger, Cudjo lifted his chin and looked down his nose at the cabin's occupants. "I reckon that crippled nigger you've got in there will just have to scrabble around on one crutch for a spell, old woman!"

Curiosity got the better of Jim, and he opened his eyes a slit and moved his head so he could see around the corner of the cabin. Cudjo's profile was etched by white moonlight, the lines of his face as hard as chiseled granite. He held his body erect, a posture that spoke volumes about his cold and imperious character. Try as he might, Jim could not find the slightest hint of compassion in the man.

Cudjo was speaking again. There was no laughter in his voice now, not even the mocking kind. "You just think about what I've said, old woman." He spit onto the ground as though to rid his mouth of a bad taste. "Three days. That's what I'll give yuh." He held up three fingers for emphasis. "And don't try none of your trickery on me, you old witch, 'cause if you do, I'll take it out of that little nigger's hide!"

Careless of the dry grasses surrounding the cabin, Cudjo flicked the stub of his cigar onto the ground. It missed Jim's bare foot by inches.

With the sounds of Cudjo's derisive laughter reverberating through the darkness, he disappeared into the long shadows of the loblolly pines.

Jim hesitated only a moment to be sure that he was unnoticed, then crept silently along the trail behind Cudjo. His mess of fish forgotten, he failed to spot the shiny black eyes of the little masked creature who watched him from a clump of scrub palmettos.

Content that the troublesome humans had other matters to attend to, the mother raccoon lumbered out of her hiding place and sidled up to inspect Jim's catch. This was a rare sight indeed: a fish dinner hanging from a tree limb! Well, no point in questioning providence. If that's the way fish were coming these days, who was she to question? With one quick swipe of her agile front paws, Mother Raccoon had Jim's fish to ground level. Stopping only to take a last whiff of the repulsive smell of humanity, the sharp-eyed thief grasped the fish in her mouth and headed home to feed her hungry family.

Cudjo seemed in a rare good humor, for he whistled and sang all the way to his quarters. He had managed to continue in the master's good graces. It had been nearly two years now since he had been rewarded with a small but quite comfortable cabin abutting the southeastern lawn of the Big House. It stood on a low knoll and had been built upon pilings, so its flooring stayed dry in the dampest of weather. A stand of southern pines sheltered its far side, and the fallen needles made a fragrant carpet around the structure that Cudjo found much to his liking.

There was a good tabby fireplace and chimney attached to the cabin. On the front side facing the Big House itself was a narrow porch lined with a sturdy railing. Cudjo had managed to commandeer one of the wooden rocking chairs from the piazza of the Big House. It sat on his front porch now, waiting for him to settle down for a relaxing hour or two before he retired for the night.

Sitting in a rocking chair, however, was the last thing on Cudjo's mind this particular evening. He wanted to make one last check of his hidden evidence. It was not a matter of being certain that the remaining crutch and the incriminating slate were still there. He knew they would be. Rather, he wanted the opportunity to gloat over his good fortune and his intelligent management of this affair of business. In his mind's eye, he could already see himself in the exalted position of plantation overseer.

Gullah Jim waited in the dark shadows at the edge of the woods until he was sure it was safe to make a run for it across the open space and up the pine-covered knoll. A nearly full, but still waxing moon was scudding in and out of a growing cloud cover. Moving as silently as a fox, the old man loped up the knoll, threw himself to the ground, and rolled partway under the open space below the cabin's flooring.

He could hear above him the heavy tread of Cudjo's feet. There was a scraping sound, then a thump as if a boot had been dropped. When the sounds were repeated, Jim knew he could breathe easier. Cudjo must be settling down for the night. Jim's mind began to race, searching for an idea that might alter the driver's well-laid plans. He couldn't best this young buck with a show of physical force. No, if he were to have any chance at all, he'd have to fight cunning with cunning.

Jim lay silent and listened to the noises above him. Cudjo must be stirring up the fire now, for he could hear a scratching noise at the base of the chimney. Then to Jim's surprise, there was a loud creaking sound in the floorboards, followed by the appearance of a thin flash of orange light just to the left of his head. Rolling over to get a better look, he caught sight of a large, dark object set into the ground under the flickering beam of light. A box! Yes, that's just what it was—with a trap door in the flooring just above it.

Cudjo's voice was distinct now. He was singing again, though there were no real words, only a discordant crowing sound. No doubt about it, the slave driver was mightily pleased with himself. A second or two passed; then there was a scrabbling noise as though something had been lifted from the box. Jim waited breathlessly in the ensuing silence.

In a deferential tone that was obviously feigned, Cudjo addressed himself to an imaginary listener. "Yessuh, massa, suh. Ol' Cudjo be mighty 'bliged ta he'ps you out wheresomeber he ken!" His mocking laughter tumbled through the hole in the flooring until Jim felt that despite the coolness of the night air, he would surely suffocate.

A sudden, loud thud against the box brought him to his senses. There was the scraping noise of loose floorboards being slid into place while the stream of flickering light gave way to darkness. The padding sounds of Cudjo's bare feet muffled by the floorboards continued for several minutes more. Finally all was quiet.

Jim had all he could do not to laugh out loud. This pompous fool was making things too easy! It took all the sport from the hunt. But then again, was it really that easy? Did knowing where the child's crutch and slate lay hidden really further Jim's hopes of foiling such a despicable plot?

The old man's heart sank. No, perhaps not. Cudjo merely had to go to the master and tell him what he'd found, and the threat to Angel's survival would remain. This trouble would need a lot more thought before the night was out.

Slithering along the ground until he had distanced himself from the slave driver's dwelling, Jim stretched his old bones, then pushed himself to an upright position. His mind tumbled one idea around after another as he walked back to Maum Beezie's cabin.

Strangely enough, he found that his appetite had returned and with it the vision of stewed mullets lying on a bed of fluffy rice. He began scouting the woods for the tree where he'd hung his mess of fish. The raccoon prints in the disturbed ground, however, quickly told him that his dream was not going to materialize on this night.

Disappointed, he walked to the cabin's doorway and tapped lightly on its exterior. Then, so as not to frighten Beezie into thinking that Cudjo had returned, he called out her name. Before entering the cabin, he made the decision that he would say nothing to the old woman of his eavesdropping or the discovery of Cudjo's hiding place. The less she knew about his own plans, the better. While Maum Beezie would surely welcome his will-ingness to assist, Jim felt quite certain that she'd not approve of the direction his mind was now working.

Morning dawned bright and clear. The rising sun found Gullah Jim well on his way down the wide expanse of the Coosaw River. On this occasion, however, he stayed clear of the swift-flowing waters of the main channel. Having reefed his sail, he was industriously poling his bateau as close to the shoreline as she would go without actually scraping her bottom. He had sighted something along here a few months ago, something that would normally have kept him well away from this shoreline in the future. But not now. Now it was imperative that he find it again.

Striking his pole against the ragged edges of an oyster bed, he scanned the bank ahead carefully. Yes, there was the half-submerged palmetto trunk and the washed-away embankment. He had found the right spot.

Pushing the bateau onto the muddy shoreline, Jim reached down and picked up his old beaver hat. He perched it atop his head of grizzled white hair and gave it an extra pat to anchor it down. Next to his boat, this hat was Jim's most prized possession. He had found it floating downriver one day, its rim bobbing along in the sunshine just as nice as you please, as though it was off to see the world minus the head of its owner.

Jim had adopted it, and hat and fisherman had been nigh inseparable ever since. Through the years it had faded a mite, and its high top had collapsed some, but such minor flaws only lent it character. Now Jim could balance his fishing bucket on the top of his hat without catching the rough wooden staves in his kinky hair. And there was an additional feature that Jim had never even counted on. He had always been a bit on the short side, but now with the hat and bucket atop his head, he took on a more statuesque dimension.

There was no need to roll up his tattered trouser legs, for they had been pushed up above his calves for so many years that now they just seemed to stay there of their own volition. Jim stepped out into the soft "pluff mud" near the oyster bed and felt it ooze between his toes. He never tired of the comfortable feeling of soft mud against his bare feet. As a matter of fact, Jim suspected that that was exactly what the good Lord had created mud for. A man who spent his life in hard shoes, a man who never felt the joy of pluff mud squishing through his toes was poor indeed.

Of course, the overgrown field that stretched out above the embankment was a different matter. Brambles and sandburs made the walking treacherous. The soles of Jim's feet were as calloused as old leather, but sandburs were nasty little things that seemed to jump out at you and find your most tender spots. Thus, picking his way gingerly through the tall weeds and around the waving broom sedge, Jim finally made it to a bit of high ground where he could survey the surrounding territory.

The old fisherman had discovered this spot some six months ago, and the way it had happened still gave him shudders. He had been dragging a shrimp net along the sandy shallows, when he had spotted what appeared to be the rotted remains of a pine box lying half-submerged on the shoreline. As he moved closer for a better view, Jim's worst fears were suddenly realized. He had come across an old slave cemetery that was gradually being washed away by the rising surge of the river!

If Jim's superstition had gotten the better of him that day, he might have poled away as fast as he could and thus have missed the very thing that he now so desperately needed. But being a man of great curiosity, he had backtracked up the river apiece, beached his boat, and clambered out for a closer look.

Today, however, he needed more than just a closer look. So plucking up his courage, he worked his way down to the grounds of the old cemetery and began nosing about. Vines and brambles had grown over everything; wind-stunted shrubs of bayberry, yaupon, and evergreen oak were already encroaching their way into the deep depressions that marked each gravesite.

Jim pulled aside some of the vines, being careful not to step into any of the depressions. He felt certain that what he had seen six months ago must still be here. He found one or two half-rotted cypress boards, but they weren't quite what he needed. Moving closer to the eroded riverbank, he began to wonder if the rising waters had beat him to his quarry.

Wait! Over there. Yes, that must be it. Jim pushed his way through the tall grasses and sank to his knees by the jagged remains of a broken cypress pole. The carved end of the grave marker was half-buried in the muddy soil, but to Jim's great joy, the features of the carving were still intact.

Lifting the strange figurine from the dirt, he brushed it off with the tail of his shirt. What this figure with the elongated head and flattened nose represented, he wasn't quite certain. Perhaps an African deity or a symbol of some special characteristic of the deceased. It didn't really matter. What *did* matter was the fact that the carved figure on this ancient grave pole was almost identical to the one that marked the final resting place of Jeremiah, Angel's much revered grandfather.

Gullah Jim had actually considered taking Jeremiah's marker from his grave, but his fear of offending the spirit of the man who had once been his best friend brought a quick end to the idea. He knew the Gullah folk often put some of the deceased's personal items on top of the grave to keep the spirit from coming back in search of such possessions. To remove one of those items was sacrilege of the worst order. The wrath of the incensed spirit would surely be visited upon the thief.

Jim was hopeful, however, that the spirit was long gone from this old marker. Surely Cudjo would never go down to the present-day slave cemetery to check Jeremiah's grave. He was far too superstitious for that. Besides, this broken, half-rotted pole would have a much greater shock value.

"Lawd," prayed Jim as he tucked the grave pole into his fish net, "ah sho' don' mean no disrespec' fer de dead, but dis es one time de livin' gotta come fu'st. Angel, she gwanna be in pow'ful trouble effen dat Cudjo don't get a piece ob he own med'cine. Reserbes oona's judgment fer does what deserbes et de most an' fergib a po' ol' fishamans fer walkin' off wid dis grabe pole."

He looked down at the deep depression in the muddy soil and tipped his hat. "Whosomeber oona be down dere, ah axes oona's pardon. Jes set tight an', soon's ah ken, ah bring dis back."

The day was well-advanced and the field hands were industriously bent over their hoe handles, loosening the soil around the long rows of cotton. Jim could hear the rhythmic words of their song as the workers chanted in time with the steady chopping sounds of the hoes:

We will all sing tugeddah on dat day.
We will all sing tugeddah on dat day.
An' ah fall upon ma knees,
An' face de risin' sun,
Oh, Lawd, hab mussy on me.[*]

Cudjo, as usual, had stationed himself under the shade of a tree at the edge of the field. His white shirt, neatly pressed by one of the laundry women just the night before, stood in stark contrast to the muted browns of the dusty field and the ragged gray clothing of the slaves. The white shirt was Cudjo's trademark, his mantel of authority. Knowing how vital that authority was to the smooth running of his plantation, the master had willingly provided his head slave driver with the necessary attire.

To Cudjo, the shirt was a matter of pride mixed with a healthy helping of vanity. But the black men and women who labored under his watchful eye unconsciously put a different meaning to it. The white shirt became a second skin that could be put on or taken off at the discretion of its wearer. Thus a black man might transform himself, at least partially, to the superior status of a white man. And with the addition of a coiled bullwhip tucked neatly into his belt, there were few who would question this alteration in his status.

With his long legs spraddled wide and his muscular arms crossed over his chest, Cudjo looked every bit the authoritarian figure. Watching him from a distance, Jim could almost feel a flicker of admiration for the young driver. If nothing else, Cudjo was a worthy adversary.

Allowing the drift of the current to carry his boat to the shoreline, Jim anchored the small craft to a log and stepped out as though he had nothing more on his mind than a leisurely stroll. It wouldn't do to call attention to himself at this point, so he left the grave marker wrapped securely in his fish net and puttered around with his sail.

The field hands were used to seeing Jim coming and going on his own. One or two of them lifted their hands to wave a greeting. Jim returned their salutations, then, with a forced casualness, balanced his bucket on his head and hoisted his net over his shoulder. As he walked up the trail from the river landing, he stopped once to adjust the net so it would hang to his right side away from the prying eyes of those working in the cotton field.

Once above the stand of live oaks, he turned back to be certain that he was well out of Cudjo's line of vision. Feeling sure that the driver could no longer see him, Jim veered off the path and headed for the wooden cabin perched atop the pine-covered knoll. He skirted around to the back of it, for there was one more "refinement" that he wished to add to this surprise he was cooking up for Cudjo.

There had been no rain for several weeks. With the warm days and the intense sunlight , the stagnant waters of the small ponds and drainage ditches were now coated with a thick layer of green algae. One such brackish depository lay just behind Cudjo's cabin. Jim eyed it with speculation. Yes, it was the very thing he needed!

After a quick look around to be sure that no one was

watching, he lifted the bucket from the top of his hat and dipped it into the algae-covered pond. By skimming the surface, he found that he could collect enough of the vile-looking slime to almost fill his bucket. The afternoon was noisy with the buzz of bluebottle flies and the constant grating sounds of cicadas. Mosquitoes nipped at the old man's bare arms and legs. He ignored them. Intent on completing his task as swiftly as possible, he made his way to the shadowed rear of the cabin, where he lowered the bucket and fish net to the ground. As long as he was careful not to unduly disturb the ground, its thick bed of pine needles would both cushion his sounds and prevent the leaving of any telltale footprints.

Jim made one last survey of the plantation grounds. Satisfied that he was unobserved, he dropped to his stomach and began working himself under the floorboards of the cabin. The air was musty with dust and decayed leaves. Granules of sand worked their way into his eyes and nose. Fighting the urge to sneeze, he crawled slowly forward.

Yes, there was the box, a sturdy-looking structure securely wedged into the space between two parallel floor joists. Jim realized that he would have to position himself between those joists if he wished to reach in and pull out the crutch and slate. Dust motes danced in the beams of sunlight filtering through the ragged edges of the cabin. In the revealing light of day, the old man began to experience the sinking feeling that this task he had set out to accomplish might prove to be more than he could handle. But he would not give up now. Surely there must be a way.

After positioning himself directly in front of the box, he reached up and grasped its two nearest corners. Perhaps he could get enough leverage to slide it out into the open. The weight of the object, however, amazed him; he could not budge it an inch. This was obviously more than a simple wooden crate. It must surely be lined with some type of metal.

Jim tried lifting his right arm as high as it would go in order to work his hand through the narrow space between the top of the box and the underside of the floorboards. The strain on his shoulder was almost unbearable. Managing to get his hand and forearm over the lip of the box, he turned himself sideways in an effort to find an angle he could comfortably work at. A sharp stabbing sensation in his upper shoulder made him jerk his arm down to his side as though he had been hit by a red-hot poker. Reaching for the throbbing shoulder with his opposite hand, the old man could feel the ragged edges of a large wooden splinter protruding from a tear in his shirt. The splinter must have come loose from one of the rough wooden beams. The sharp end of the projectile had pierced both his shirt and the skin underneath.

Clucking with frustration, the old man crawled out from under the cabin. A thin rivulet of blood spiraled down his arm and dripped onto the carpet of pine needles. The splinter had gone deeper than he thought. Sitting cross-legged on the remnants of an old stump, he tried to pull out the offending bit of wood, but it was so far to the back of his shoulder that he could work only by feel rather than sight.

There was nothing he could do now but leave the splinter and go on with his intended task. Working with a dogged determination, he unwound his fish net from the grave marker and turned the pole over in his hand to examine the carving. The wooden eyes seemed to stare angrily back at him, as though incensed at such disrespectful usage. Jim shuddered but slid the pole under the cabin. Finally he placed the bucket of slime in the dry sand and dropped to his stomach once more.

By first pushing the pole ahead, then slithering sideways to pull the bucket forward, he laboriously managed to inch himself back into position. Movement was harder this time, for the wound in his shoulder was stinging unmercifully, and his entire right arm seemed to be growing stiff. To make matters worse, he couldn't reach far enough into the box to feel either the crutch or the slate.

Then an idea struck him. Using his uninjured left arm and hand, he began to dig away at the soft, dry sand at the bottom edge of the box. It wasn't long before he had created a large enough depression to tip the heavy crate down so he could peer inside. There lay the crutch in plain sight. The slate was there also, but Cudjo had carefully wrapped it in an old piece of oilcloth, obviously to prevent the chalked lettering from being accidently rubbed off.

Jim wasted no time in removing the items and putting the grave marker in its place. The marker was slightly longer than the box, but that didn't matter. Jamming it in at an angle so the carved end stood higher than the base, the old man pulled his head back and critically examined the effect. Yes, it looked about right. Now for the slime!

It took three bucketfuls of the putrid liquid to fill the box sufficiently so that only the face of the carving peered out from the clinging layers of slime. Jim had been right; the box was fitted with a copper lining, making it quite watertight.

After dumping the last bucket of algae-filled water over the marker, Jim felt exhausted. He rested his head and arms on the sand for some time. He was lying there quietly when he heard the clip-clop sounds of a horse's hooves in the distance. By turning his head sideways, he could just make out the erect figure of Master Weldon sitting astride Diablo, his big roan stallion.

Horse and rider stood perfectly still, both of them alert to their surroundings. The master seemed to look directly at the base of the small cabin where Jim lay hiding. Could he possibly have been spotted?

Unconsciously, the old man held his breath, though such an action would add nothing to his concealment. Then he realized that the master was simply scanning the landscape. It was something he had a habit of doing. From that distance, however, it would be quite impossible to make out the figure of a man lying in the crawl space under a cabin.

Jim waited until the master jerked at the reins and urged his mount down the trail that led to the cotton fields before he once more lifted his head and shoulders. This time, without tipping the box, he managed to work his head up high enough so he could peer into its dimly lighted interior. A long, admiring gasp escaped his lips. The effect was perfect—absolutely perfect!

---

* Ballanta-Taylor, p. 67.

8
Dark Side of Night

(1860)

Satan, wa da fight gainst oona, da gwine all obade place, same likka hongry lion, fa find somebody he kin graf hol ob (1 Peter 5:8b).

Cudjo arrived at his cabin late that night. Having pilfered a bottle of Jamaican rum from the master's personal supply, he had been doing a bit of celebrating. Nothing serious, just enough to make him feel relaxed and a bit lightheaded.

The interior of the cabin was pitch black, for he had forgotten to bank the fire that morning. Groping about for his flint and iron, he overestimated his reach and painfully scraped his knuckles on the rough exterior of the tabby fireplace. Shaking his hand to stop the throbbing pain, he let out a string of curses. This wouldn't have happened if he hadn't forgotten his lantern. The worst part of it was, he had no idea where he had left it.

The pain in his hand sobered him some. It wasn't long before he got the fire going again. He had used several pine cones as tinder. Every so often one of them would explode into a shower of hot sparks that lighted up the room and sent eerie shadows dancing along the walls.

The noises of the exploding cones made Cudjo feel jumpy. After adding several oak logs to the fire, he began pacing the room. He had the oddest sensation that he was not alone. Must be the liquor, he decided. Reaching for the half-empty bottle, he ran his fingers over the strange markings on the label. What did they mean? He would like to know. Could he really blame that little crippled nigger for wanting to learn to read and write?

He took another long swig from the bottle and wiped his mouth with the back of his hand. Given half the chance, he'd jump at the opportunity to get a bit of book learning. "That's what separates me from the white master in his Big House," he mumbled into his hand. "Book learnin'—knowin' how to read and write—how to figure sums."

Grasping the bottle with both hands, he examined the label carefully. He broke a small twig from a piece of kindling and began to trace the outline of each symbol. Was this what the child did as she marked on her slate?

Bah! What did it matter what she did? A lot of good her book learning would do her anyway. She was a slave and a cripple, good for nothing. And why should he care what might happen to the child if he revealed her secret? Uppity, that's what she was, both she and her grandmother. But he'd take them down a peg or two. He'd show them that all their kowtowing to the buckra— "Yessuh, massa. No, suh, massa"—would get them nowhere. And what if they did learn to make sense out of all these symbols? Would that really make them equal to their white masters? Cudjo laughed derisively. No! Never! The only thing that whites really understood was the business end of a pistol.

Tipping the bottle up, Cudjo took another long swallow. How strange, the more he stared at the symbols on the label, the larger they became. In fact, they seemed to be moving, constantly pulsing and undulating as they grew larger.

Perhaps it was the smoke from the fire. Yes, something must be partially blocking the chimney. Half in a stupor now, Cudjo sensed that there were thin columns of smoke rising from the hearth and filling the room. He rubbed at his eyes and tried once more to trace the strange symbols on the label, but for some reason they were disappearing. Where? Where would they go?

Wait. There they were, in the column of smoke. Still growing, they coiled around the dark shadows of the ceiling and began to change, taking on the elusive images of living things.

Cudjo felt himself begin to tremble. This liquor was no good for him. It put ideas in his head, made him see things that weren't really there. Or were they? Lifting the bottle angrily, he heaved it across the room toward the fireplace. It hit the mantel and broke into a thousand pieces, spilling its contents onto the floor in front of the hearth. Instantaneously a dragon leaped from the smoky interior of the fireplace, licking up the spilled liquid as he came, then belching it back out in a spray of searing flames. With his arm shielding his face, Cudjo jumped backward. The room seemed to be alive with all manner of creatures. They perched on the rafters and glared down at him, their eyes like burning coals and their breath hot on the back of his neck. He tried to back away, but he smashed into his table and sent a stack of wooden plates clattering to the floor.

Overcome by his drunken imagination, Cudjo braced himself against the wall and made his way slowly to the door. The night had turned cool and damp. A misty rain was blowing off the river, bringing with it the tangy taste of the sea. Cudjo sucked in air like a drowning man. He fell against the rail and retched up some of the rum. Dropping into his rocking chair, he forced his eyes closed and tried to relax. His body was an empty cotton sack.

"I'll sleeb a while," he mumbled, the slurred sound of his own voice ringing in his ears. "Sleeb—jush slee—"

Cudjo's head sank onto his chest. He never even felt the cold, misty rain as it settled in his hair and gradually soaked through his clothing. A screech owl screamed in the distance. The field hands in their quarters heard it and shivered, fearful that the ghosts of their restless ancestors were coming back up the river with the sweeping gusts of wind.

It was still several hours before sunrise when Cudjo awoke. His teeth were chattering and his body was shaking as though he'd taken ill with yellow fever. Dropping his head into his hands, he tried to recall why he was sitting on his porch in such vile weather. A vision of some strange, weaving symbols flitted through the back of his mind like disturbed bats in a darkened cave.

Grasping the railing with both hands, he tried to pull himself to his feet. He must get out of this rain. Why, he was soaked to the bone. No wonder he was shivering so!

He had to stand there several minutes before the trees and lawn stopped reeling. Feeling his knees buckle, the driver leaned hard on the rail. This was no way to act when he was about to gain such an important victory. He'd go into his cabin, get some dry clothes on, then take one more look at that crippled girl's slate. There was something there he needed to see. Now what could it have been? Oh, yes, the symbols. Cudjo had no idea why they were so important. Perhaps when he looked at them, he'd remember.

The interior of the cabin was smoky, but the embers of the dying fire were still visible in the hearth. Cudjo walked unsteadily toward their warm glow. He picked up the iron poker and prodded the coals to life, then added a few more logs.

He needed something hot to drink. There was no more coffee, not the real kind. The master was getting rather tightfisted of late. Fortunately, Cudjo had learned the ancient Indian art of brewing a stringent black drink from the cassena berries that grew so prolifically on the Sea Islands. He hung a potful of the inky mixture over the fire and went to change into something dry.

The wind was howling through the chimney, and sheets of rain battered against the windows. The storm had worsened since Cudjo had entered the cabin. He could hear branches scraping against the outer walls. An occasional pine cone torn loose by the wind dropped onto the roof with a loud thud. Cudjo felt the edgy feeling coming back. Having pulled off his boots, he walked barefooted back toward the fireplace.

Unprepared for the sharp splinters of glass scattered in front of the hearth, the driver walked into them with the full force of his weight on the balls of his bare feet. Letting out a shrill yowl, he tried to find a clear spot of flooring that would not bring back the needlepoints of pain.

He needed no further stimulant to sober him. Ignoring the bubbling pot of cassena drink, he sprawled across his bed and tried to pick out the most offensive slivers of glass. Things were not going the way they should. If Cudjo didn't know better, he would swear that someone had cast a voodoo spell on him. Surely that child's witch of a grandmother wouldn't try to cross him like this! Or would she?

Enough of these games. Gritting his teeth against the pain, Cudjo pulled his wet boots back on and made his way toward the loose floorboards and his secret compartment. He'd show that vicious old woman that two could play this game as easily as one. Why, when he finished with that crippled nigger girl, the old women would be glad to be rid of her!

Cudjo slid the boards away. After gingerly feeling the floor for flecks of glass, he dropped to his knees. Odd, it seemed especially dark down there in the box. He leaned over and dropped his right hand and arm into the hole. Grasping something wet and slimy, he jerked his arm back in alarm. Could the box have somehow leaked?

He looked down at his right hand and shuddered. The hair on the back of his neck felt as though it were crawling. What was this stuff all over his hand? It seemed to be congealing as it dried in the warm air of his cabin.

Desperate now to see if the crutch and slate were still there, but too repulsed by the slimy interior of the box to reach back in with his hand, Cudjo pushed himself upright and walked toward the fire. He lifted one of the thicker kindling logs from the pile and pushed it into the flames. What on earth had he done with his lantern? His actions of the night before seemed to be shrouded in a bank of thick fog.

With the burning kindling as a torch, he made his way back to the hole in the flooring. Straddling the open space, he lifted the torch high and tried to make out what was in the box. The dawning certainty that neither the crutch nor slate was there filled him with a new kind of dread. Something *was* in there, and that was for certain.

Dropping once more to his knees, he slowly brought the torch closer to the hole. Its flickering tongues of fire wavered in the cold draft coming up through the open flooring. And to Cudjo's dismay, the damp wind also brought with it the strange images from his drunken delirium. Not really wanting to see the quivering thing that lay in his box, but strangely driven to it by his relentless fear of the unknown, Cudjo moved his face closer to the hole.

A piercing scream split the night, shattering the sleep of those in the slave community who dreaded the coming of such a stormy morning.

Maum Beezie was just heading out her door on the way to the Big House when she heard the clatter. It seemed to be coming from Cudjo's old cabin down on the other end of the quarters. Strange. It had been sitting empty for months. Who could be moving in at this time of the morning?

"Angel, honey, oona jes' wait hey're a spell. Ah has a li'l somepun ah got's ta do afor ah leabes fer de Big House."

She didn't really. It was pure curiosity. No one in his right mind would want to move into Cudjo's old place. It had a bad smell to it. Not the kind you sniffed with your nose. Something worse, like a hot breeze off the marshes that carried with it the threat of sickness.

Angel smiled and waved. What a good child she was! No. Maum Beezie wasn't going to lose her, no matter what Cudjo said. She'd go to the master herself, tell him everything, plead with him if she had to. She'd learned to grovel a long time ago. That was one of the first lessons you learned as a slave. She'd do it for the child, no matter how bad it hurt her pride.

Coming around the corner of a cabin, she wasn't prepared for the sight that met her eyes. Blue paint splattered everywhere! And Cudjo up on a ladder with a brushful of the stuff. It ran down his arms in ragged streaks, matching the hurried brushfuls he'd slopped around the door and window frames.

Cudjo didn't hear her coming. He looked awful—like he'd seen a ghost. His hair was matted and his white shirt was almost unrecognizable. His face, the part she could see of it, was full of long, hollow lines. He was working as though the very devil was after him.

Deciding that this was as good a time as any, the old woman walked up to the base of the ladder and pulled on one of Cudjo's pant legs. She had it on her mind to tell him that she was going to the master this morning. She was *certain* that she'd tell him about her decision to have no part of his blackmail scheme.

Cudjo shifted his weight and looked down at her. His face went ashen gray. "Get away from me, you old hag!" he yelled, and almost fell off the ladder.[1]

A splotch of blue paint flew from Cudjo's brush and hit Maum Beezie in the face. She rubbed it off, then examined her hand. Blue paint around the windows and doors! The realization of what Cudjo was doing suddenly struck her. She should have known right away. It was an old Gullah belief, part of the ritual to ward off spirits. Cudjo thought he was being haunted by an angry ghost. Now where would he have gotten such an idea? More to the point, where had he gotten that blue paint? Stolen from the master, more than likely. That was the way Cudjo got most everything.

"Cudjo, ah comes ta tells oona—" She started, but never finished the sentence.

"Get away from me, you hag! I don't care if I never see you again. Look here, we'll make a deal. You just stay clear of me, and I won't say a thing to the master about your grandchild breakin' the law."

"Don' matter nebersomehow," answered the old woman. "Et's me what's goin' ta de massa fu'st. Goin' right now, afor he heads out ta de fiel's."

The whites of Cudjo's eyes grew large with fear. "You gwanna tell him about last night, about what I said to you?"

"Nope, reckon not. Reckon der es nough t'ings chasin' oona's tail widoutten de massa tryin' ta pin he up fer a whippin'."

She'd keep that promise too, though she knew she probably shouldn't. Cudjo *needed* to get caught. But then, the coon who got away with stealing from the Big House usually tried again. It was only a matter of time before the master would get wise to his high jinks and set out his own traps.

Cudjo looked relieved. He felt more relieved when Maum Beezie turned and walked away. "She's a witch, no doubt about it!" he said under his breath. How she'd conjured her dead husband's grave marker into that box was a mystery, but she'd done it. It was bad enough to have the living after him. Having the dead breathing down his neck was more than Cudjo could handle.

Angel was struggling around on one crutch when Maum Beezie came back for her. She was trying her best to straighten the place up.

"Honey, chil', afor weuns goes ta de Big House, dere es sumpin' oona an' Maum Beezie's gots ta talk 'bout."

Angel hung her head and waited.

"Don't get dat hang-dog look 'pon yo face, chil'. What oona done was right, no matter what de white man's law say. An' don't oona neber let a polecat de likes ob Cudjo scare yo. Dat man es all mean, right down ta he toes. Meanness like-a-dat hab got a way ob festeren inside. Purty soon de whole body es full ob pizzon. Et's sumpin' like when a pusson steps 'pon a rusty nail. Get de pizzon out which ebersomeway oona ken. When oona see a red line climbin' up de leg, et's way too late."

A look of sadness crossed the old woman's face. "Dat's de way et es wid Cudjo, honey chil'—way too late. De red line hab gone too far—all de way ta he haid. De pizzon's gone ta he brains an' es startin' ta fester. Now he be scared ob ebery shadow—see t'ings what ain't eben dere." She shook her head sadly and turned away. "Too late fer Cudjo," she mumbled under her breath. "May de good Lawd hab mussy 'pon he soul!"

They arrived at the Big House just as the master was finishing his breakfast. He'd been out in the fields since sunup. Returning to the Big House, he'd decided to catch up on his missed breakfast before starting on the pile of paperwork awaiting him in his office.

Maum Beezie passed Cudjo's erstwhile "new" cabin not the least bit surprised to find that he'd securely boarded it up. What the master would make of that was anybody's guess, but the problem was for Cudjo to deal with. The old woman snorted with contempt. He might also have to explain the smell of stale liquor that seemed to radiate from the place.

"Massa Weldon?"

The master looked up from his breakfast plate and smiled at the elderly nurse standing before him. Her dress and shoes were damp from walking through the wet woods. She stood a bit crooked, as though the arthritis in her knees was throwing her off balance. Gilbert felt something inside of him soften. He would just as soon she stayed in her own room here at the Big House each night. He'd done his best to fix it up comfortably for her. It was certainly warmer and drier than her own drafty cabin, with its cold dirt flooring.

But she'd been adamant in her refusal. It had been her decision to return to the quarters after the day's work was done, and he'd respected her for it. "What's good 'nuff fer de field hands es good 'nuff fer weuns," she'd explained in her own inimitable way. As best he could tell, it had something to do with giving Angel a sense of community. Besides, she was much needed in the quarters for her nursing skills, and she was doing her best to teach Angel those same arts of medicine and healing. The child, though a cripple, was already a great help to her elderly grandmother.

"Massa Weldon—me an' Angel—we gots sumpin' what needs tellin'."

The master set down his fork, noticing for the first time the small black girl pressed against her grandmother's skirts. The old woman's face looked drawn. Whatever it was she had to say was serious. He'd not make it harder for her. Nodding, he waited for her to continue.

"You knows dat ah lobes dis chil' mor'n ah lobes mah own life. An' ah' lobes yo' chillun too—lobes em like dey were mah own." She hesitated, waiting for him to respond.

"Yes, Maum Beezie. Your love for them is unquestioned. If there's something wrong—something worrying you—just tell me. You know that I'll do whatever I can to help."

"Ain't he'p weuns needs now, jes understandin'. Angel—well, suh—she's kinna grown up wid Laura May, an' sometimes she jes don' know de diff'rence. She don' know dat dere be certain t'ings fer white folks, an' udder t'ings fer colored folk."

She swallowed hard. Gilbert could see the tiny beads of sweat on her brow grow bigger. There was something in what she was saying that made him feel uncomfortable. He was good to his people, but he always made certain that they knew where the lines were drawn.

"Take laws, fer zample," she continued. "Dere be some laws fer white folk, an' udder laws fer colored folk. Most eberybody knows dat. But—well, suh—sometimes a li'l chil' don' know dat."

Now Gilbert felt alarmed. Laws? What was she getting at? Without realizing what he was doing, he reached for his table knife and began pressing its handle into his hand. "Maum Beezie, I think you better tell me right out," he said, tension lacing his voice and making it sound sterner than he really wanted it to sound.

"When Mister Thorne come here an' starts fer ta teach Laura May all dat book learnin', well, et jes seem ta make sumpin' snap inside mah Angel. She hear 'bout all dem good t'ings what Laura May findin' in dem books. Habin' twisted feet like she hab, dere be a passle ob t'ings what she jes kyan't do. But a pusson don't need straight feet fer book learnin'. Jes takes good eyes an' a good haid ob brains. Now dat be two t'ings what mah Angel habs— good eyes an' good brains."

Master Weldon held up his hand to stop the old woman's explanation. He had heard enough to tell him all he needed to know. Now he understood the empty spaces in the bookshelves of his library, the scraggly, half-washed-away letters he had seen on the beach, and that good leather-bound version of Longfellow that had been so carelessly left in the hayloft. He wanted to smile, but that rigid law about not teaching slaves to read and write seemed to pull his mouth the wrong way.

He looked at the small black child and saw that she was transfixed in place by fear. Her grandmother was silent, but there was a resolute look on her face. It spoke not of fear, but of great courage. In that moment Gilbert gained something of a clearer vision. It was as though the blinders of wealth and privilege had momentarily dropped away from the sides of his face, allowing him to see the world beyond the walls of his own comfortable homes.

Setting down his knife, he pushed his chair away from the table. He walked to the foot of the stairs, looked upward, and called for Laura May. She came skipping down, taking the stairs two at a time. When she saw Maum Beezie and Angel, her face blossomed with happiness. Unaware of their tense postures, she flung herself into the old woman's waiting arms and put out a hand to include Angel.

"You're late this morning, Maum Beezie," she said, with feigned adultlike severity. "I finished my breakfast, and I'm all ready for my classwork with Mister Thorne."

Maum Beezie glanced up at the top step. Mister Thorne had come to see what the commotion was about. He stood there smiling down at her. The tutor had liked Maum Beezie from the first day of his arrival.

Master Weldon motioned for Aldis to come downstairs. "This is a matter that concerns you as much as it does me," he said, his voice still veiled over with sternness. "We have a problem that needs solving. They say that two heads are often better than one, so perhaps you can think of some helpful suggestions."

Aldis Thorne came down the stairs with the dignity of his station evident in each careful step. The ragged black ribbon that hung from one side of his pince-nez glasses swayed back and forth as he descended. He held his chin high, so he was forced to let his spectacles slide down on the bridge of his nose in order to see over their tops. Maum Beezie noticed that despite Josephine's good cooking, the tutor hadn't put on an ounce of weight. It was as though he burned up his food, not with physical labor, but with the glowing fire in his brain.

At the master's direction, the small party went into the study and stationed themselves around his desk. Gilbert chose not to seat himself, however. He'd remain standing with the others; this was no time to pull rank.

With the greatest of care, he explained the laws that had been passed forbidding slaves to learn to read and write. "Do you understand the purpose of those laws?" he asked the group in general.

Everyone but Aldis Thorne nodded. The tutor just stood there, his mouth drawn into a tight line and his eyes full of thunder. It was more than obvious that he approved neither of the laws nor their purpose.

Gilbert Weldon turned to face the teacher head on. "Mister Thorne, what you think of slavery is your own affair. What you think of me as a slaveholder, however, is my affair. This country is changing; I hardly have to tell you that. There are fissures developing between the North and South that may well be irreparable. Knowing these things full well before you accepted this position, you still chose to come South."

Aldis started to speak, but Gilbert held up his hand. "There's no need for you to explain why, Mister Thorne. I respect your decision, and I am grateful for it. You've done an admirable job with my daughter, sir. The question is, can you do an equally good job with this black child?"

The shock of his words turned the room into a sepulcher of silence. Aldis's spectacles fell from his nose. Not even the sound of breathing could be heard.

"Well, sir, what do you say?" asked Gilbert, his face still serious and stern.

"I—ah, I—I don't quite understand what you mean." For the first time in his life, Aldis felt entirely tongue-tied.

"I thought I said it quite plainly, sir," answered Gilbert. "Can you teach a Negro child to read and write?" He reached over, and with both hands, picked up the family Bible. "Are you able to teach her to read this book? I've always felt that the Holy Scriptures is the best place to start, perhaps more so for a child with so many burdens to bear."

"I—why—yes, I suppose I could," stuttered Aldis.

"It shouldn't be hard, my good man. From what I understand, she's already got the rudiments of learning."

He turned to face Maum Beezie and saw the tears rolling down her cheeks. Flustered by the sight, Gilbert cleared his throat loudly and pulled his growing smile back into a stern line. "A word of warning, however. What we have said—ahem—what I have said must go no further. Mister Thorne will follow my instructions, but I have *not* given him a license to educate every black pickaninny in the quarters. I will not hold with the flagrant breaking of the law."

Clearing his throat again, Gilbert looked slightly embarrassed. It was not easy for him to show softheartedness. "You of course realize that I'm making an exception with Angel, for, in a way, I consider her a part of this family. Her companionship brings pleasure to Laura May—and—and I want my daughter to be happy." Hardening the lines of his face into a scowl, Gilbert's voice grew tense. "Does everyone understand my meaning?" he asked with a firmness that no one could mistake.

Once again, there was a general nodding of heads. And this time even Aldis Thorne enthusiastically joined in.

"Now then," Gilbert sat down at his desk matter of factly, "I have work to do." It was quite obvious that everyone was summarily dismissed.

The shadows of evening had already gobbled up much of the woodland when Gullah Jim came back to Maum Beezie's cabin. He had no string of mullets with him this time, only a sheepish grin and a badly festering right shoulder. And there was one thing more; he had Angel's other crutch. Having considered the slate far too incriminating, Jim had taken it out to the center of the river for disposal.

Maum Beezie pulled away Jim's shirt and clucked her tongue with concern. "Oona in de habit ob walkin' inta wood splinters, Jim?" she asked quietly.

"Spec' mah boat, she gettin' a mite raggidy 'round she edges, Beezie. Reckon ah es gwanna hab ta smooth she out a spec."

"An' dis crutch? Where oona find um? Floatin' down de riber, mayhap?"

"Why, bless mah soul, no, Beezie honey. Found dat crutch lyin' in a blackberry patch. Spec Angel lost um, so's ah brung um straight back hey're."

"Oona 'straight backs' hab a way ob wigglin' round in some mighty big circles, Jim." Beezie fixed him in place with her naughty-child frown. "Now et's mighty good fa folkses ta wanna he'p one annuda, but some t'ings—well, suh—ets jes better ta leab um in de hands ob de Lawd."

The old woman smiled and patted Jim's hands, but then she grew serious again. "An' unnder t'ing needs sayin'. Dere's a wickedy slabe driber wa done spent a mighty haad night fighten' wid de debil. Now he bring some ob dat 'pon hese'f, an' dat fa true! Howsomeber, der seem ta be a trickstah in de woodwuk conjurin' up a haunt wa doan need conjurin'. Oona know sumpin bout dat, Jim?"

Jim cleared his throat and looked at the ceiling. "Member wa Jeremiah used ta say, Beezie? He say, 'Onpossible ta get straight wood from crooker timber.'" Then, despite the painful throbbing of his shoulder, Jim broke out into a mischievous chuckle.

"Um-hmm, dat wa he say," answered the elderly woman. "But ah also recollects Jeremiah sayin' a word er two 'bout sumpin' called pre-sumption," she added, this time with a certain stern-ness to her voice. "Now oona lissen ta wa dis ol' 'omans got ta say, Jim. Gawd don't need peoples runnin' off ta de debil ta do He wuk. Oona be one ob de finest men ah knows, Jim, but ah hab tol' you a hund'ed times dat ah doan want no truck wid hoodoo er black magic!"

Jim shrugged his shoulders. "Ain't neider hoodoo ner black magic ah was usin', Beezie. Jes a pinch ob common sense. Effen a man's conscience needs a prick now an' den, ain't nuttin' wrong wid ol' Jim bein' de pin. Ain't dat what a preacher do when he commences fer ta shout 'bout de Lawd's retrebution?"

Maum Beezie shook her head sadly. Jim was a good friend, and she didn't want to hurt him, but she couldn't leave the argument where it lay. "De Lawd's retrebution es one t'ing, Jim. Howsomeber, when et gets mixed up wid man's retrebution—well, suh—dats askin' fer de debil ta pit in he hand. Sumpin like mixin' sour milk wid good cream—turns de whole bucket bad!"

Jim nodded his understanding. "Oona's a good woman, Beezie. Dat li'l gel Angel es a mighty lucky chil'!"

Maum Beezie pressed a poultice to Jim's shoulder to draw out the puss. "Dat li'l gel's got sumpin' a lot bigger den de likes ob dis ol' 'omans, Jim. She gots de good Lawd lookin' after she!"

Jim circled his shoulder around and rubbed at the numbness in his hand. He stood up and turned around to face the elderly nurse. Placing his calloused hands on her shoulders, he smiled into her face. "Nex' time oona an' de Lawd converse, Maum Beezie, oona be sure ta t'ank He fer gibin' weuns de bestes' nu'se in de whole Souf."

Pulling her face toward his, Jim kissed the woman lightly on her forehead. "An' one t'ing more," he added. "Asks de Lawd effen He ken forgibe a po' ol' fishamans fer actin' like a hard-shell quayhog[2]." The fire flickered low in the hearth as the two elderly people sat and watched its ebb. Hard times were coming, but they still had their friendship. That was enough for now.

---

1. *Hag* is the Gullah term for witch.
2. *Quayhog* is a large Atlantic shellfish.

9
Thunder Rolling

(1860)

God gwine laan we E way so dat we kin waak een E road
(Isaiah 2:3).

S tuffing his son's letter into his coat pocket, Gilbert
nodded to the boatmen and stepped onto the dock. It
was a clear day in early October, with just the hint of a
misty rain far to the northeast. A cool breeze rippled the river's
surface, delicately brushing it with golden flecks of sunshine.
Dappled circles of light filtered through the trees and fell onto
the soft grass along the shore like coins dropping from a
tattered purse.

On any other such day the master would have been filled with
contentment, for the weather seemed to mirror the wealth of
cotton growing so prolifically in his fields. But there was no joy
in his heart, not now. His son's latest letter had destroyed it.

Stopping as though to examine something at his feet, Gilbert
waited until the boatmen were well out of sight before he
slumped to the ground and pressed his back against the trunk of
a sheltering oak. A deep weariness lay upon him, an exhaustion
of the spirit that physical rest could not relieve. He had felt it
coming on for some time but had pushed it away with the
impatience of a man too busy to be bothered by a troubled mind.

Had he mistaken the tone of Gilly's words, taken them too
personally? Perhaps his own concerns for the direction the
country was going had altered his ability to think objectively.

Pulling the letter from his pocket, he smoothed the paper against his thigh and reread the opening lines:

Dear Father,

Please keep this letter from Mama and Laura May, for I do not wish to worry them unnecessarily. Perhaps I have become overly pessimistic in regard to the escalation of political tensions, but I think not. The truth is, my mind has been very troubled of late. I respect your opinions, Father, and despite our past differences feel that I can share my concerns with you.

There is a growing undercurrent of anger and mistrust here at the naval academy that must certainly reflect the general mood of the nation. Men who once served together, who fought side by side to uphold this country's honor, are now at odds over the most basic of constitutional rights. Among Southerners, talk of secession is running rampant. Northerners, on the other hand, remain totally intolerant of the South's difficult economic position in this new industrial age.

My fear is that the growing animosities threaten to undermine the foundations of not only this institution, but the very nation for which it was established.

You must understand that as a lowly fourth classman, I am hardly privy to the talk in the officers' mess. Word, however, does filter down to us from time to time. Little of it is good. There are southern men among both the officers and midshipmen who have emphatically stated that they will leave the academy if Mr. Lincoln is elected to the presidency this November. My studies keep me far too busy to allow for careful scrutiny of the candidates' platforms, but. . . .

The letter went on to describe the very same kind of talk that Gilbert had been reading just last week in the *Charleston Daily Courier*. The gist of that article now came back to him with a startling reality. There was a new militancy in the country: men marching with banners and torches, shouting inflammatory slogans, and wearing clothing that could easily pass for military attire. Perhaps none of them were more enthusiastic than a popular band of Republican youth called the Wide-Awakes.

Gilbert had clipped out the article about them along with an artist's sketch of their parade after the Republican's Wigwam convention in Chicago.[*]

Pressing his head into his hands, Gilbert closed his eyes and sucked in a deep breath of air. He felt old. He was barely forty-four, but age had somehow crept up on him, lining his face with deep furrows and brushing the hair at his temples with wide streaks of gray. Dropping his hands to the lapels of his coat, he pulled them tightly across his chest. The air seemed to be growing colder. Perhaps that rain shower he had seen in the distance was heading this way. He clamped his teeth tightly shut to ward off the tremor that was creeping across his shoulder blades.

Young men marching, and when he closed his eyes every one of them had Gilly's face. What had he done? He had been a fool! He had relented, given in to his son's insistence that he be allowed to attend the naval academy. And now there were young Northerners marching with black capes on their backs and split rails over their shoulders looking for all the world like an invading army. Nor was the North alone in this militaristic fervor. Talk of secession and states' rights swept across the South like an advancing storm, carrying with it the distant thunder of rumbling caissons.

No, he must not think this way. Surely there would not be a war, not here on American soil, where the blood of patriots had nourished the high ideals of brotherhood and liberty! Surely there were still men of reason whose rational opinions would prevail!

But try as he might, Gilbert could not push away the vision of impending conflict. It *was* coming. He could feel it in his bones; age had nothing to do with it. It was like a deep infection not yet festered but ready to burst with the slightest pressure. And Gilbert must face it head on, not for himself or even for his wife and daughter. They would be safe enough, thank God. There were no armies foolish enough to fight over these insignificant, mosquito-infested Sea Islands. No, he must face the reality of war for the sake of his son, for it would be his generation that would bear the brunt of it.

And with the fear of losing his son to the bloody specter of war, a new revelation came upon Gilbert that brought with it both physical and emotional pain. He had seldom showed affection for his son; he knew that. Gilly was too different, too out of step with the society he had been born into. He had a way about him that rubbed a man raw, especially an authoritative man like Gilbert. Father and son had been constantly at odds with one another, but despite all that, Gilbert loved his son more than he loved his own life! And now, only now, the force of that realization had come home to him.

Slumping his shoulders, Gilbert let his head drop back against the trunk of the oak. A spot of sunlight touched his face, blessing it momentarily with warmth. How he longed to digest its warmth, if only to slow the quaking of his body. But even as he sat there, the bit of sunlight disappeared. Then the chill came again, stronger this time. Not bothering to clamp his teeth against the tremor that coursed through him like an electric shock, Gilbert gave himself over to its violence. And now it felt good, this penitence for opportunities missed and words unsaid. The cold steel of pain and the trembling muscles were his sackcloth and ashes.

How long he sat there, he did not know, but finally the world came back into focus. Letting his eyes drop once more to the letter in his lap, Gilbert searched for the few ambivalent lines that gave him both comfort and regret:

I know that you were much against my coming here in the first place, Father. Thus, I am sincerely indebted to you for granting me the privilege of accepting this appointment. In your wisdom and judgment you felt that I should remain on our land so that I might one day fill your shoes. It will, therefore, probably come as good news that I may soon be forced to make the painful decision of leaving the academy to return home. The very thought of that, however, fills me with unspeakable sorrow for . . .

Gilbert didn't need to read the rest; he knew it by heart. And if there was a tone of bitter resentment to this letter, it was understandable. Gilly had had such high expectations. Young people always did. Fearing war, they could march into its very teeth with a whistle on their lips and a glint of adventure in their eyes.

Resting the palm of his hand on the letter, Gilbert allowed his gaze to float with his thoughts across the bright expanse of the Coosaw River. Could he share any of this with the boy's mother? Yes, perhaps some of it. She deserved to know that her son had found some measure of fulfillment.

With a tongue-in-cheek style, Gilly had described life at Annapolis. Discipline was rigid, but not unbearable. He had made friends. He was doing well in his studies. He missed the gentle climate of the Sea Islands. He missed Maum Beezie's tenderness and Josephine's cooking. And he missed his family. Yes, that was what Marian must know; her son truly missed her.

Gilbert tried to look at Gilly's latest news in a positive way. Perhaps the altercations within the school's officer corps would shake out the misfits and malcontents. And if the political maneuvering of a nation itching to divide itself brought his son back home, he would not complain. But would this really change anything? It certainly wouldn't alter Gilly's resentment of being confined to a few acres of cotton land. Nor would it change the rocky road the nation seemed bent on breaking its axle on.

Gilbert waited while another tremor passed. Perhaps he was coming down with something after all. The weather had been changeable lately. A man could easily catch a chill when, rain or shine, he must spend his days in the open fields. He should get himself up to the house. Perhaps Maum Beezie could stir up one of her concoctions, which would make him feel more like his old self.

Instead of moving, however, he continued to sit and stare at the river. The words of Gilly's letter kept rummaging through his mind: ". . . if Mr. Lincoln is elected to the presidency . . . careful scrutiny of the candidates' platforms . . ." Without a doubt, Abraham Lincoln seemed to be the hinge pin of this whole controversy. This time Gilbert's shudder was voluntary. The thought of seeing that gangly Rail-Splitter from Illinois sitting in the White House was appalling!

Gilbert clenched his fists and pressed them against his forehead. His thoughts were running about like a flock of chickens with the fox after them. He had to pull himself together. What if someone found him like this? Crumpling the letter into a tight ball, he wadded it back into his pocket.

Pushing himself upright, Gilbert methodically brushed the leaves and grass from his trousers. He jerked down the lower edge of his coat to straighten his lapels, then lifted his head high and walked up the shaded trail that led to the stables. A man couldn't be too careful about appearances when he had a plantation full of slaves watching for his every slip.

As he approached the paddock to the north of the stables, Gilbert noted that Samuel and Zach were working with one of the carriage horses. Zach, his legs spread wide and his face lined with concern, had ahold of the horse's bridle with one hand while his other hand lay reassuringly on its neck.

Samuel, the head groom, was at the animal's rump with one of its legs bent up so he could examine the hoof. They'd had a lot of rain lately; the pastures were a quagmire. If the horse came down with hoof rot, there would be reason for concern. But that was for Samuel to worry over. He was every bit as good with horses as Jeremiah had been. Besides, Gilbert certainly didn't need another problem added to his already overtaxed mind.

Watching the two young bucks, Gilbert felt some of his depression lifting. They made a good pair, those two. Putting them together had been one of his better ideas.

Zach's despondency after his young master's departure for Annapolis was a point that still rankled in Gilbert's mind. There was no doubt but that he owed the young black man something. Though a questionable house servant, Gilbert had to admit that Zach had been an excellent companion for his son. They had learned a lot from each other, but it was most often Zach who had kept things on the straight and even.

Sending the young Negro away from the Big House after Gilly's departure hadn't been easy. But what else could he have done? Gilly had hardly been gone a day before Marian was on Zach like a she-bear with a tick in her ear. For the life of him, Gilbert couldn't understand why his wife was so dead set against the boy. She had never really explained it, but just pointed her finger to her head and said, "Woman's intuition!"

Perhaps she resented Zach because he hadn't been born on the place. Funny, Marian sometimes acted like the people in the quarters were her own children. She never did tolerate outsiders well. The fact that she had finally accepted Aldis Thorne was nothing short of miraculous. Northerners, as far as Marian was concerned, were a pariah to the human race. Gilbert chuckled to himself. If it ever did come to war, the South would do well to enlist Marian into its ranks as quickly as possible!

Gilbert felt better. His dark mood was lifting. Perhaps he should tell Zach about Gilly's letter. Not the political part, of course. The less the slaves knew of such things the better. But then again, Gilbert could not help but wonder if they already knew more than they let on. He trusted his people, but he was no fool. They certainly didn't work his land out of gratitude.

Leaning on a fence post, Gilbert watched as Zach backed the big horse closer to the stable door. The young black had a firm but gentle way with the animal. No doubt about it; he was proving himself to be a capable stable boy. Even Diablo, as mean as he was, tolerated Zach's attentions.

Yes, perhaps he could share just a few things from Gilly's letter with Zach. For instance, the black boy might get a real kick out of hearing about some of the hazing a cadet had to go through as a new midshipman. Gilly's description of the dressing down he'd gotten for having a smudge on his right shoe would certainly set Zach to howling with laughter. The young servant would understand that sort of thing, would probably even empathize with it. Hadn't he had his own share of dressing downs?

Not that Gilbert had ever been that hard on Zach. Well, maybe a little. Maybe he had taken some of his frustration and anger out on the boy. But that was natural. Something to be expected. Gilbert couldn't help but think of Zach as an extension of Gilly himself.

It was just then that Zach looked up and saw the master standing by the fence post watching him. Clearing his throat to get Samuel's attention, he nodded his head slightly in the master's direction and rolled his eyes in warning.

Samuel spun around, his face sharp with a startled expression

that for a split second of time contained a hint of fear. "Mornin',
Massa Wel'on. Wasn't 'spectin' you back so soon. Sumpin' happin'
dat bring you back early?"

Gilbert looked at his groom critically. "Now that's a strange
question for a servant to be asking his master," he said, with
irritation in his voice. "And what business is it of yours if I choose
to come home early?"

Samuel touched his hand to his forehead and looked properly
repentant. "Didn' mean no disrespect, suh. Tain't none of mah
bus'ness at all. No, suh, tain't mah bus'ness at all."

Gilbert pushed open the gate and walked into the paddock.
Unless he'd suddenly lost his ability to judge the bowings and
scrapings of these niggers, there was something nasty brewing
nearby. His glance slid over to Zach, who stood transfixed in the
barn doorway as though he had seen a ghost.

"Well, boy, did that horse stomp on your foot, or is your mouth
hanging open just for the fun of it?"

Zach's eyelids fluttered up as though he had been startled
awake from a deep sleep. "No, suh, *Massa Weldon*, suh," he
answered, the sound level of his voice rising as he spoke the
master's name. "Horse ain't stepped on mah foot. *No, suh, Massa
Weldon, suh!*"

And on the last "Massa Weldon," he turned his face toward the
open barn door. Then reaching up toward the horse's ears, he
busied himself with the bridle straps and began a toneless sort
of whistle as though the whole matter was none of his concern.
Gilbert's sharp eyes, however, had caught the trembling in the
young man's hands and sensed a warning signal in his whistling.

There was a sudden scurrying sound coming from inside the
barn, and then the padding of little feet on the hard-packed
ground at the far doorway. Spinning around to look back at the
path leading to the quarters, Gilbert saw a dozen or more woolly
black heads duck under the fence and disappear.

"What's going on here?" Gilbert demanded. He pushed his way
past Samuel, who had suddenly stepped in front of him as though
to block his passage. Walking with long, determined strides, he
stepped into the dimly lighted interior of the barn. It took several
seconds for his eyes to adjust to the darkness, but when they did,

he was shocked to see the tall, gangly form of Aldis Thorne coming down the ladder from the hayloft. Clouds of dust and bits of hay, disturbed by the sudden passage of smaller bodies, floated lazily down through the shafts of sunlight that filtered through the cracks of the barn's siding.

Aldis did not hurry. He came down the rough-hewn rungs as though he was cautiously making his way down the steps of a library ladder. Upon reaching the bottom, he made a studied effort at picking out hayseeds and bits of straw imbedded in the coarse wool of his coat. Then lifting himself to his full height, he adjusted his glasses on his beaklike nose and peered at the plantation master over their wire rims.

"I suppose you have an explanation for this, Mister Thorne?" asked Gilbert, his voice icy with controlled anger. His eyes riveted to the small bundle of slates tucked under the tutor's right arm.

Aldis glanced down at the slates as though noticing them for the first time. "Yes, Mister Weldon, I do indeed have an explanation."

"Then perhaps you might consider sharing it with me," Gilbert continued, his eyes moving up to the tutor's face.

"I am a teacher, sir, a man trained and dedicated to guide the minds of the young—"

"Yes, indeed. I do recall that," Gilbert interrupted. "It happens to be one of the reasons I hired you. Now perhaps you could enlighten me further as to why you chose such an unlikely place as the hayloft of my barn for your classroom. One would think that you had something to hide!"

Gilbert waited, but Aldis gave him a level look and remained silent. "Haven't I gone out of my way to provide a more than adequate classroom in the Big House? In fact, I even granted you the liberty of using the piazza when the heat became too excessive in the house. Why, then, may I ask, have you resorted to the barn?"

"As I was saying, Mr. Weldon—" Aldis didn't seem the least bit phased by Gilbert's building rage. "Ahem—as I was saying, I am a trained teacher dedicated to bringing education and enlightenment to the young, who—"

Gilbert grated his teeth in frustration and slammed his fist against a nearby post. "Blast you, Thorne! I didn't hire you to come down here and educate my pickaninnies. I hired you to tutor my daughter. I paid your passage here—first class, I might remind you—and have been paying you a handsome sum in the bargain. I've opened my home, as though you were one of the family, and entrusted you with my child's welfare."

Aldis raised his hand, pleading for a chance to speak. "And I am grateful to you for all of that, sir. I have not failed in the duties given to me, nor have I betrayed your trust. Your daughter has a quick mind and a passion for learning. I have systematically endeavored to—"

Gilbert's eyes were the mirrors of his rage. He moved his face close to Aldis's and threw out his words with such force that their sound waves seemed almost visible. "You, sir, have *systematically* gone behind my back to advance your own warped concepts of educating ignorant black slaves! You and your fine abolitionist friends have used me as a dupe, betrayed my trust in you, and seduced my family into thinking you had nothing but their best interests at heart!"

Aldis's face worked with anger and then softened. He reached out one hand and placed it on Gilbert's trembling shoulder. "I do have their best interests at heart, Gilbert," he said quietly. "Yours, too, I might add."

Gilbert reached up and threw the tutor's hand from his shoulder. "I've not given you leave to address me on a first-name basis, Mr. Thorne." He stepped a pace backward and brushed at his shoulder as though to rid himself of the leavings of some vile insect. "That is a privilege I grant only to those whom I consider my friends."

"But I would like to be your friend," persisted the tutor. "This country is gnawing at its own insides, cannibalizing itself with hatred and mistrust. Surely, you and I can stem the tide just a bit by refusing to be a party to such madness."

"This country, Mister Thorne, has seen fit to pass legislation prohibiting the education of black slaves. When you set yourself above those laws, you place everyone around you in grave jeopardy: me, my daughter, my servants, and yes, even those pickaninnies you are trying so hard to enlighten. We've discussed this once before, and my instructions on the matter were clear. I made an exception for Angel because I know I can protect her. I cannot, however, protect every slave who comes and goes on my plantation. Do you know what they do to niggers who break the law, Mr. Thorne?"

Aldis drew himself up tall. Tight lines pulled at the corners of his mouth. "I know a great deal about the cruelty and injustices of mankind, Mr. Weldon. I've seen more than my share of them. Somehow, I thought that you and your family were different. Somehow I thought that you had risen above the prejudices that turn grown men into ravenous wolves."

Gilbert's voice, though still tense with anger, lost some of its edge. "I do not make the laws, Mr. Thorne. As a good citizen, however, I am sworn to uphold them. What you do not seem to realize is that there are rational reasons for such legislation. Education can be both a tool and a weapon. In the wrong hands, it can bring untold suffering and even bloodshed. If we keep our slaves ignorant, we do so out of compassion for their childlike ways and their—"

Now it was Aldis who interrupted, his face no longer able to hide the anger growing within him. "*Compassion? Compassion, you say?*" His voice rose to a shrill crescendo. "Compassion for whom? No, Mr. Weldon, you've chosen the wrong word. Conceit would be better, or even greed, but *never* compassion. You keep these poor souls ignorant, for you know perfectly well that they would not labor in your fields from sunrise to sunset and live in the hovels of your slave quarters if they had the slightest insight as to what they were really capable of.

"You claim paternalistic love for them while you pump them of their very life. Their infants and children die of disease and malnutrition, their young men and women are bartered and sold like common beasts of the field, and their old—those who somehow survive to be so classified—are so crippled from overexposure and utter exhaustion that they can barely tend to their own bodily needs."

Gilbert's face grew livid with rage. "*How dare you! How dare you slander me so!* My people are like my own family. Look at Maum Beezie, Gullah Jim, Josephine—trusted servants, every one. And I treat them all with the deepest of respect and compassion."

"You treat them well only because they *are* servants to your own family!" Aldis hissed out the words through clenched teeth. "If they served no useful function in your household, Master Weldon, they'd be out in the fields with the others, beasts of burden to be used and then thrown aside."

Shaking with the passion of his rage, Gilbert had all he could do to keep himself from smashing his fists into the tutor's ghastly face. "*Get out of my house!*" he shouted. "Get out tonight! Pack your bags and be as far away from here as you can by sunset, or I'll have you lynched from one of my own oaks!"

Spinning around on his heels, Gilbert stormed from the barn. Samuel and Zach were standing in stunned silence just beyond the doorway. They had never in their lives witnessed such a flood of untamed hatred. Gilbert turned on them as though to vent the remnants of his rage, but then held himself in check. "You two have obviously had a hand in this, now, haven't you?" he asked, the bitterness of his words lashing out at them.

Neither one of them answered. Their faces were ashen with fear, and the whites of their eyes showed vividly against the black of their faces. Rivulets of sweat rolled down their cheeks.

"They had no part in it other than holding their silence, Mr. Weldon." Aldis had followed Gilbert outside and stood now with his arms akimbo and his face stern with determination. "Surely you would not take out your anger on trusted servants who are like your own family! Leave them be. I will do as you say. I will leave your house and your property this very afternoon."

Gilbert spat onto the ground and then turned to face Zach head on. "Saddle Diablo, boy, and be quick about it! I need the feel of fresh air on my face. The smell of vermin has fouled the air hereabouts."

Zach disappeared into the stables and came out minutes later, leading the massive stallion. Sensing the fear and anger around him, the horse laid back his ears. Pale lines encircled his eyes. He sidled about nervously, jerking and chewing at the bit. Gilbert mounted the great beast in one fluid motion and viciously slapped the looped reins against the animal's neck as he lifted himself up in the stirrups. With his nostrils wide and his muscular front legs flailing the air, Diablo reared. Zach released his grip and fell to the earth, instinctively rolling his body into a tight ball to protect himself from the slashing hooves.

Oblivious to the fear and discomfort of his mount and his servants, Gilbert wheeled the horse around and took off across the paddock with the pounding of hooves. A cloud of dust and sand rose in his wake. As horse and rider approached the fence, Gilbert gave a vicious kick to the animal's flanks. The horse lifted into the air, clearing the topmost rail with a good twelve inches to spare.

Never once did he turn his head to look at the startled line of field hands moving methodically along the rows of cotton. Never once did he notice the two frightened girl children, one black and the other white, cowering under the fence rail at the far end of the paddock. For Gilbert Weldon—the war had begun.

---

* Bruce Catton, *The Coming Fury* (Garden City, N.J.: Doubleday, 1961), p. 89.

10
We'll Stand the Storm

(1860)

Ain't notin too haad fa God ta do (Genesis 18:14a).

The flag that flew over Charleston harbor on the morning of November 7, 1860, was not the Stars and Stripes. A deep blue banner boasting a white palmetto tree and crescent moon had been hoisted up the pole as soon as the results of the presidential election reached the city. To the people of Charleston, that simple act marked the birth of a new nation. The oft-repeated pledge ". . . one nation, under God, indivisible . . ." had lost its meaning. Division had come, and with it, jubilation—at least for the present.

A large crowd of citizens gathered on the Battery to cheer this symbol of their newfound loyalty. They hung from the lampposts and stuck jaunty blue cockades in their hatbands while congratulating themselves for keeping the very name of Abraham Lincoln from their polling booths. It did not matter, of course; no true Southerner would have voted for him anyway.[1]

The Boston steamer standing in the harbor swung about on its anchor line and gave the Palmetto flag a fifteen-gun salute.[2] The sounds reverberated across the water, echoing the scattered but exuberant bursts of gunfire erupting from the Battery. Bracing himself against the rail of the steamer's upper deck, Aldis Thorne, the tails of his threadbare coat whipping in the wind, bowed his head into his hands and wept. Never before had he felt so completely overcome by his emotions. Worse yet, never before

149

had he felt such a desire to weep over something he could not completely comprehend. Was he crying for a state seceding from a nation or for a single family turning away from the one virtue that would have made it a cohesive unit?

Slipping his hand into the deep inner pockets of his coat, Aldis's fingers touched the worn copy of the small New Testament he always carried with him. He had no need to look up the text that came to mind as he thought of this family's greatest need; he had learned the words by heart years ago:

> Though I speak with the tongues of men
>   and of angels,
> And have not [love],
> I am become as sounding brass,
>   or a tinkling cymbal.[3]

As he stared down into the choppy surge that made the ship pitch and roll on its anchor line, a watery memory of the family came before him with a special sadness.

He would never see them again, of that he was certain. Had he become confused in his priorities? To be fair to them, perhaps he should have revealed his Quaker beliefs and abolitionist loyalties. His northern brethren openly opposed the heinous crime of slavery, but all too often they did so from the comfort of their parlors' armchairs. That was not for Aldis. If the warfare was to be joined, it must be done on the battlefield. He would not sit on the sidelines. And to him, the cause must always come before the individual. Slavery in all its vile forms must be stamped from the face of the earth. Aldis knew that in the battle for the human mind, the weaponry of education was of too great a value to be sacrificed to his personal feelings for one family. But he would miss them. Yes, he would miss all of them.

A scraggly line of pelicans followed the steamer past the newly bricked walls and casements of Fort Sumter, standing sentinel-like at Charleston's gateway to the sea. Aldis, still riveted to the deck while he watched the receding skyline of this most genteel of southern cities, felt a sudden surge of elation. His mission had not been in vain. He had planted the seed. Its germination was certain. Even now he could sense that the small scene he had just witnessed was but a minute part of something greater still to come. The sun glinted off the tall, clean spires of Charleston's churches. The city's elegant houses, with their pastel walls and filigreed iron railings, slowly blended into the haze, transforming the entire scene into a washed-out watercolor. Somehow the rock and brick walls of the new fort seemed too hard, too forbidding for such a soft background.

Then Aldis's eye caught the rippling Stars and Stripes that flew above Sumter's ramparts. Pride welled up within him. He caught his breath and stood erect. Pulling his hat from his head, he placed his hand upon his chest in silent tribute and felt the pounding of his own heart. The steady beat of it gave him new courage. Perhaps he would come back some day to this southern shoreline. Perhaps his personal involvement in the battle for freedom was not yet over.

By the time the steamer reached the outer channel, the growing haze had turned into a salty mist that settled like silver dust on the worn cuffs and collar of the tutor's woolen coat. For one brief moment the man looked polished. The soft smile that slowly crept across his face gave him a carefree appearance, covering the hot passion that burned in his eyes as he thought of the work still to be done. He turned from the rail and headed toward his cabin as the mainland faded away into the misty skyline.

Some eighty miles to the south, another man turned his back on the dark waters of the outgoing tide and walked bent shouldered toward his home. Unlike Aldis Thorne, however, there was neither cheerfulness nor zeal to buoy his steps. Gilbert Weldon felt beaten. His young daughter, the very joy of his life, once again lay in a sickbed that threatened to turn into a deathbed. Although the fever that had ravaged her small body and burned the very flesh from her bones had abated, she remained delirious and weak with exhaustion.

Rising before dawn the next day, Gilbert had boarded Gullah Jim's skiff and traveled all the way into Beaufort in search of a physician. Dr. Barnes, harried by a recent outbreak of scarlet fever, tried to put off the distraught father with a bottle of quinine and some simple words of reassurance. "Mister Weldon," he said in his most professional tone, "the child has had dozens of these attacks and will likely have dozens more. One must simply be patient and wait till they pass."

"She needs neither quinine nor a patient father, sir," answered Gilbert angrily. "The child is at death's door. I've never before seen her quite so taken by these recurring fevers and chills. It's as though she no longer cares to fight them."

"And your colored mammy, can she do nothing? From what I know of that woman, she's quite capable." Dr. Barnes tucked the quinine bottle into Gilbert's pocket.

"Maum Beezie is a capable nurse, but she is not a physician," answered Gilbert, frustration making his voice sound tight. "We've gone over this ground before. Her ignorance exceeds her knowledge on such matters as this. Look here, Barnes, we're talking about a white child—my daughter. This is *not* a pickaninny from the quarters!" Gilbert's hot temper had reached its boiling point. "How much do you want?" Pulling a wad of bills from his hip pocket, he slammed them onto the physician's desk.

Dr. Barnes looked disdainfully down at the bills, lifted them up, and placed them back in Gilbert's shaking hands. "It is not a question of money, Gilbert," he said, in a controlled but compassionate manner. "I *will* come out and see your daughter, but you must wait until I've made my morning rounds. Go back to your town house and try to relax a bit. I'll meet you on the docks before the turn of the tide."

The trip back to Coosaw was interminable for Gilbert. The skiff had never seemed so slow, and the outgoing current had never seemed so sluggish. Even the birds in the sky appeared to hover in place. It was as though time itself held its breath, while the angel of death moved with rapid efficiency.

It was late afternoon when they finally arrived. Dr. Barnes barred the frantic parents from their daughter's room while he made his examination. He approached Laura May with professional detachment: taking the rates of her pulse and respiration, pressing his stethoscope to her chest and back, spreading her eyelids to examine the pupils. The burning heat of her last fever had been replaced by an overpowering chill. The shaking of the child's small frame was so great that even the heavy wooden bedstead quaked.

Dr. Barnes had seen all of this many times before. What he had not seen, however, certainly not in the case of this favored white child, was the look of utter despair in her clouded eyes. The father was right; the will to live had gone out of her. And if the cause for such hopeless resignation was not soon resolved, the spirit of life would go out of her too. Packing his instruments back into his bag, Dr. Barnes shook his head sadly. He had no medications for this malady. Nor was he even sure that he had the right words. Try as he might, this was always the most difficult part of his profession. He had escorted many a child into this world, but he still dreaded the act of escorting one out.

"She needs more than I am capable of giving her," he said as he touched Marian's trembling hands with his strong but delicate fingers. "There is, however, a greater physician than I, Mrs. Weldon. He is the one you must turn to now." Reaching for his clean white hanky, Dr. Barnes gently wiped away the tears that slid unchecked down Marian's cheeks. "Go and sit with her for a while, my dear. The worst of her fever is over for the present. She may be too weak to talk, but I believe she's lucid enough to hear you."

He put his arm around Marian's sagging shoulders and helped her back into the sickroom. Seating her in the rocking chair that stood beside the bed, he gently tucked a comforter around her legs. "I promise to come back tomorrow, though it may be late before I can do so. But listen to me, Marian: you, too, need your rest. Have one of the house servants send up the child's mammy within the hour so that you can get to bed. I'll give you something to help you sleep."

Marian waved him away weakly. "No, no. We mustn't do that. Maum Beezie is too crippled with rheumatism. She can barely walk. I've sent her back to her place in the quarters so her granddaughter might care for her."

"Hmm, I see." The doctor's brow furrowed in thought. "Perhaps I'll take the time to go down to the quarters before I leave. It wouldn't hurt for me to have a look at her."

Flickering yellow lamplight spilled onto the carpeted floor of the hallway as the physician stepped quietly from the room. Gilbert Weldon moved across the beam of light, his shadow casting a momentary darkness into the already dismal hall. "Well, can you do nothing more than deepen our discouragement? Surely you have some medicine, some procedure—"

"Gilbert!" Grasping the father's arm with his strong hands, Dr. Barnes led him away from the open doorway. "Let's go down to your study. There are some matters that I must discuss with you." And without waiting for a reply, he led Gilbert firmly down the stairs. The study door was open, and a neglected fire burned low in the grate.

Leading Gilbert to an easy chair, the physician turned and poked the fire's embers back into life, threw in another log, and then propped himself on the desktop with one leg straddling its corner. There was a strained silence as he examined the cluttered desktop. Then, though unbidden to do so, he reached over and picked up Gilbert's journal, which lay open with the pen on its face as though the last entry had been unfinished.

"Does this contain some clue, Gilbert?" asked the physician quietly.

"I beg your pardon?" Gilbert glanced up at the doctor in bewilderment.

"Is there a clue in this journal you keep as to why your daughter has lost the will to live?"

Gilbert, startled by the doctor's bluntness, was left speechless.

"Something has turned her from a carefree child into an emotionless invalid. The spark has gone from her. Is there anything in this journal that can shed some light on what, for the present, seems so inexplicable?" The physician's gentle bedside manner was gone. He bore down on the planter with a relentlessness that kept him pressed against the back of his seat.

"I'll tell you this but once, Mister Weldon; if we don't come to the bottom of this quandary right soon, you may well pay for it with your daughter's life! I can treat the child's body, but I cannot heal her soul."

Gilbert slid forward and dropped his head into his hands. His shoulders heaved with the wrenching sobs that he could no longer contain. "It's my fault—all my fault. I'm a feckless fool incapable of showing affection to those I love the most!" Hesitating, Gilbert wrung his hands in agony. The realization of what he had done to his family was almost more painful than he could bear.

Dr. Barnes, sympathetic as always to pain, let his voice grow soft. "Your love for your daughter is most evident, Gilbert. You mustn't be that hard on yourself."

"No. No. You—you don't understand, doctor." Gilbert looked up into the physician's face as though pleading for understanding. "It was selfish, you see—selfish love—the kind that smothers. I realize that now. She—she's always been such a giving child. She felt pain when I showered my love upon her and had none for anyone else. Angel—Maum Beezie's crippled granddaughter—Laura delighted in giving to that child."

The words came spilling out now, heedless of what they might reveal. "And her tutor—Aldis Thorne—she had to share him too. She knew he had turned my hayloft into a classroom for pickaninnies. Why, bless me, I'll warrant she helped supply the books!"

The doctor looked at Gilbert with confused eyes. In seeking to unstop a bottle, he had broken a dam. But his professional judgment told him that he must not interrupt. This flood was of a cathartic nature, necessary to the healing process. And no matter what he heard, whatever the master of Weldon Oaks might reveal, he'd keep it to himself.

"Yes, I've failed Laura May—God knows I've failed her. She wanted my love, but not at the expense of others. Sharing comes second nature to her. But the worst of it is—I've failed my son. I turned away from him because he refused my attempts to recreate him into my own image."

The anguish on Gilbert's face was now so acute that the physician reached out and gave him a reassuring pat on the knee.

But the flood of self-recrimination continued. "I've lost him," Gilbert moaned. "I've lost him as surely as I'm losing Laura May. And I'm losing Marian, too, though that is something that entirely escapes me. Perhaps this life we've been building together is too much for her. Perhaps her mind is too frail to withstand the constant trauma."

Looking once more into the physician's eyes, Gilbert's call for help was as tragic as it was sincere. "What can I do, Doctor? What can I do? Perhaps it's too late—too hopeless—like trying to stem the outgoing tide!"

Dr. Barnes slid off the desk and stepped over to stand at Gilbert's side. He placed his hand on the planter's shoulder. "No, it's not too late, Gilbert. As long as there's breath in your body and the will to change, it's never too late."

Gilbert jumped up and flung himself toward the desk. Picking up his journal, he leafed through the pages until he came to the entry that told of his firing of Aldis Thorne. He flung the open journal into the doctor's hands. "Have you heard nothing I've said? You asked for a clue? There it is, the final straw that broke my daughter's will to live."

Dr. Barnes searched Gilbert's eyes momentarily, then looked down at the proffered journal. He settled himself into Gilbert's vacated chair and quietly read the heavy-handed script that had been angrily scrawled across the page as though the pen had contained venom rather than ink.

There was a long silence, and then to Gilbert's utter astonishment the physician began to laugh. "Well, well," he chuckled. "So the fellow was a Quaker, was he? They're a zealous bunch, all right. A bit wily, mind you—but sincere. Upon my word, Gilbert, one can hardly blame you for reacting the way you did. I mean, it's like discovering that you've let the enemy camp in your kitchen while you entertained your friends in the front parlor."

"And you find that amusing?" Gilbert was incredulous. "You've made me bear my soul to you, reveal my deepest fears, and you can do nothing more than quip about the perfidy of Quakers!"

Dr. Barnes smiled up into Gilbert's angry face. "The healing of your wounds has already begun, Mister Weldon. By expressing your fears, by admitting your errors, you have exposed the infection that's been festering under the surface all these years. Now you must let it drain until it is clear of putrefaction. Rid yourself of the inhibitions that have kept you from reaching out to those you love. Learn the lessons of giving that your small daughter has so beautifully exemplified. Learn how to love your son and your wife unconditionally. In time, everything else will fall into place."

Pushing himself up from his seat, Dr. Barnes closed the journal and placed it carefully back on the desk. "I'll go down to the quarters now and have a look at Maum Beezie. Despite her age and affliction, she's a resilient woman. You have much to be thankful for, Gilbert. Not many families have the benefit of such a dedicated and wise servant."

As he started to walk from the room, Dr. Barnes hesitated, and then turned once more to face the master of Weldon Oaks. "One thing more, Gilbert. Intelligence is not a trait exclusive to the white race. The sooner you planters learn that, the better off we all will be. Wisdom, now, that's another matter. The more I see of the way things have been going of late, the more I wonder if any of us have it." Shrugging his shoulders, he turned and walked away. Gilbert went to the window and in the fading light of evening watched the doctor head down the trail leading to the slave quarters. He felt relieved somehow, as though a terrible weight had been taken from him. Perhaps repentance was good for the soul after all.

Glancing once more at his closed diary, Gilbert began to smile. Then he turned and headed for the stairway. Perhaps it was not too late. Perhaps he could still tell Laura May how much he loved her. Perhaps he could still show his wife that he was a man capable of controlling his temper. And as for Gilly, well, he'd write to the boy in the morning and let him know that his father had every confidence in him no matter what career he might choose. As he approached his daughter's room, Gilbert saw the flickering light coming from the half-opened doorway. Marian was still there, sitting just as the doctor had placed her. The deep lines of worry that had creased her forehead just moments before were gone. There was a serene smile on her lips; her vacant eyes no longer swam with tears. Gilbert sighed. His wife had retreated once more into that safe hiding place—a place where no one could follow.

The thought that he should get the tutor back crossed Gilbert's mind, but a small crust of pride still clung to his heart, and he erased the idea before it could grow. He had recognized his faults, admitted his errors, and now he must deal with their consequences in his own way. Encircling his wife's shoulders with one strong arm, he gently stroked her hair with his free hand. "I'll go to the quarters and get Maum Beezie, my sweet. Rheumatism or no, she'll not refuse me."

Marian said nothing. She was in her own secure world, protected from reality by the enclosed walls of her mind. The fact that she, too, needed the comfort and wisdom of the elderly black mammy escaped her. It did not, however, escape the master. And in his heart he was thankful that he could transfer to another the art of giving love. Maum Beezie still must be his surrogate for the time being, but perhaps he could learn.

It was as though the sound of the sea surged in her head. Laura May struggled against the fog. A light momentarily flickered and then disappeared. Cool lips touched her forehead, a hand brushed back her damp hair. Gilly's face quivered on the edge of her consciousness only to be replaced by the face of her father. The recurring words of a Negro spiritual faded in and out:

Deep river, Lawd . . .
My home is over Jordan.
Deep river . . .

Another wave washed over her and the fog rolled in. Laura May heard her own voice calling for someone, but just who it was seemed to elude her.

Deep river, Lawd.
I want to go over into . . .

Her mind drifted off into a place of sunshine. It was as though she was a sea gull gliding effortlessly through space and time. Below her she could see Coosaw sewn into a patchwork quilt of other islands. Rivers and creeks lay across the land like ribbons, with sunshine glinting as though they had been woven with threads of gold. From this height it appeared to be such a peaceful place!

Deep river, Lawd.
I want to go over into campground.[4]

Laura felt herself being drawn down. The land lost its hazy glow, the rivers and creeks ceased to glimmer in the sunshine. Details became clearer. A huddle of squalid little cabins marred the soft green of the woods. The fields were scarred with lines—too straight, too square, too unlike the gentle curves of nature. And those small insects crawling about in the furrows like worker ants, their heads bent low under their burdens. The sight of them took the last bit of buoyancy from Laura May's body. She felt herself falling toward earth. Grasping desperately at thin air, she let out a piercing scream and awoke with a start.

The warm black arms were around her—cuddling her close. "Hush, child. Hush-a-by. Maum Beezie's hey're. Maum Beezie's right hey're aside you."

Laura May opened her eyes wide and looked into the old woman's face. Behind the cracks and crevices of old skin, behind the dark pigmentation of race, there was the glow of love that knew no barrier of age or color.

Seeing the light of renewed health in the child's small face, Maum Beezie sank to her knees at the side of the bed. "Praise de Lawd! Praise de Lawd fer He kind mussies!" she shouted.

"Maum Beezie?"

"Yes, chil'?"

"Are you going away?"

"What you mean, chil'?"

"Are you going away on that deep river? Are you going away to campground?"

"No chil', not jes yet. Someday. Mayhap soon. But not jes yet."

"When you do go—will you take me with you?"

"Well, bless mah soul, chil'!" Maum Beezie's face creased into a deep, warm smile. "No, no, honey chil'. When et be mah turn to cross dat riber, you gotsta stay here fer a spell—you, and mah Angel too. Dere's work fer ya'll ta do down hey're. Hard work, chil', so you mustn' let de debil put you down none."

Pulling herself painfully up from her knees, she sat on the edge of Laura May's bed. "And Maum Beezie, she's gwanna be prayin' fer ya'll. Yes, Lawd, jes as long as ah es on dis side ob de riber, ah es gwanna be prayin' fer you."

"But—but when you do get over on the other side—into—into campground—"

Placing her worn dark hand on Laura May's small white one, the old woman let her tears flow freely. "When dat day come, chil'—when we all get ta campground—well, den, we all gwanna sit down at dat welcome table tugedda!"

"Can I sit next to you, Maum Beezie?"

"Bless mah soul, chil'! Course oona kin!"

---

1. Bruce Catton, *The Coming Fury*, p. 111.

2. Ibid.

3. 1 Corinthians 13:1.

4. James Haskins, *Black Music in America* (New York: Crowell, 1987), p. 6.